COLD WEST

CLAYTON SNYDER

Also by Clayton Snyder

Thieves' Lyric Series
River of Thieves
Thieves' War

Blackthorne
Demons, Ink
The Obsidian Psalm
The Infernal Machine

With Michael R Fletcher
Norylska Groans
A War to End All (Manifest Delusions #3)

Short Stories
Summer Souls (in Alchemy of Sorrow)
Injustice (in Three Crows Magazine Issue # 8)
Hounds (in Grimdark Magazine Issue #30)

One

They say when a man meets the love of his life, all the mean goes out of him. Sometimes in small bits, like venom leaving the blood, sometimes in great rushes like an open artery. I don't know about that. I do know when that person's gone, it starts to slip back in, a knife in the heart.

I can vouch for the fact it came back when I laid Ginny in the ground. In drips and drabs, and not right away. But sometimes the world pushes. Then it pushes a little more. And a man's got little choice but to push back.

What will they say about me when I'm gone, then? Not much, likely. He was a bastard and a liar. A rotten thief. A killer. But mostly I was fed up. And a fed-up man's got a lot of moral leeway.

It started in '72, when the wind blew cold from the Etter Peaks, snow snapping at its heels like a dog eager to please its master. Ginny had been sick. The kind that gets deep into the chest, digs around in there. Puts its fists into your lungs and squeezes. When she finally went, it was a relief. For me and the boys. They weren't much older than me when I lost my pa.

He'd been taken by the Wasting, something they'd let loose during the first war. It ate a man's insides in slow fashion, reduced him to skin and bone. Weakness, of the body and the mind, the heart and the liver. Weren't no medicine for that sort of thing, and in the end, he was little more than a skeleton. I wanted to spare my boys seeing their mother like that, but sometimes the world's got a different way of thinking from yourself.

The earth was hard and stubborn, little more than clay and rock, and we had a hard time breaking it. Took us most of two days to cut the grave into the earth while Ginny lay in her bed, under a shroud I'd made from one of her favorite sheets, sewing her up in it like a caterpillar in a cocoon. No butterfly promised here, though. Just the long sleep in earth clenched like a fist.

When we were done, we brought her out, the boys at her feet, me at her head. She was light, like a bundle of twigs, and for a moment, I was worried we might break her into a thousand fragments. The boys were brave, to their credit. I don't know how. I was nearly broken inside, all brittle and hard, winter ice on a pond. Fallon only sniffled. Carter blinked away mist from his eyes. And that was that.

We lowered her gently, the body turning in our hands despite ourselves. She twisted once, hit the side of the grave and slid into the hole. I coughed out a sob, and the boys nearly wailed. I should've let them, but you let feeling get free, and it's like to run away with you. Instead, shook my head and nodded toward the shovels.

"Gather those up, boys. We need to cover this before the

coyotes come calling."

They did so, and we shoveled dirt over my dead wife in earnest, hoping to beat the scavengers. When it was done, I tamped the surface down and threw the shovel to the side, then gathered up rocks. We placed them on top of the grave, and at its head, a slab of wood I'd carved. Simple, and easy.

Ginny Cutter
'39-'69

I stood and looked at the boys. "You wanna say sommat?" I asked.

They shook their heads and I nodded. "Go on inside, then. Leave me with her."

The boys shuffled into the house, and I stood beneath a grey sky, looking up. Finally, I took in her grave.

"Not much of one for words," I said. "I loved you. I hope it was enough."

Then I went inside.

I gathered the boys in front of the fire, rubbed the lotion Ginny kept in the cabinet on the blisters they'd earned digging her grave. Looked around.

The cabin was sparse, aside from Ginny's touches. A piece of needlepoint on the wall. A vase of wildflowers. A bright towel in the kitchen. As for me, I'd never been much of a woodworker or a carpenter. Was a bit of a shit farmer, as well. The few crops we'd managed to eke out of the plains had been the boys' doing. Brighter than their pa, they were.

I wrapped their sore hands in strips of linen, Carter giving a little hiss of pain as a blister burst, Fallon just looking at his hands. I gave them a hot bowl of stew. It was hard work, digging graves. I hoped they wouldn't have to dig another for a long while.

We sat at the splintered dinner table, quietly eating. Outside, the wind had kicked up, rattling the eaves and the shutters on the windows. The boys finished quick, no horseplay or sharp words, and excused themselves. I cleaned up, the silence in the room like the aftermath of a pistol shot, then tucked the boys in.

"Papa?" Carter asked.

"Yeah."

"Is Mummy in Heaven?"

"Yeah, yeah she is."

Fallon spoke up. "With Tracer?"

Tracer had been our old farmhound. I nodded. "Yep. Probably sitting on a porch somewhere, rocking and sewing. Just waiting for all of us." The boys looked at me with a sad mixture of hope and sorrow. I shook my head. "Long way off, yet."

"Won't she get bored?" Fallon asked.

I shook my head. "For us, it'll be a lifetime. But for your Mom, a heartbeat. Don't you worry. Now, bedtime. Chores in the morning."

I leaned in and kissed their foreheads and turned down the lantern in their room, then left, closing the door gently behind me.

Once I got them settled to bed, I wandered to my chair by the fire. I sat for a long moment, staring at Ginny's empty one. Tried not to think of the reassuring creak of the rockers against the floorboards. Looked over to the basket on the floor. A ball of yarn, needles sticking out lay in that basket, one long string trailing across the floor. More balls beneath it, mostly grays and mud daub hues, but here and there a splash of color: blue and red, for the boys.

I turned away, sought out the bottle of whiskey I'd hidden behind the vase of flowers on the lintel. Stupid place to hide it. I knew she knew about it. Never said anything. She believed in letting a man have a vice, in small doses, knew taking away his pleasures all at once brought out the venom. I pulled it down, tugged the cork out with my teeth. Spat it to the side. The stuff was strong, the scent scorching my nostrils. I took a deep swallow, let it burn its way down my throat. Coughed. Took another pull. Fell into my chair, my head swimming.

Man starts drinking, he starts to thinking. Not that those thoughts always make sense, and certainly not good sense. I remembered the first time I'd met Ginny. I'd been with— what was the name of that company? The name swam away from me, swam back. The Free Blades. We'd been commissioned to root out some minor lord or other from his holdfast. Was taking up too much of the local duke's land and livestock.

We were on the way back from that, bloody, sweaty, and lusty when we stopped in some nameless village. And there she was. I won't lie and tell you she was a great beauty. But she was solid. And no-nonsense. It took her all of five minutes to cut through my bullshit. Maybe another ten to get me to promise to come back at the end of my commission. And I did.

I suppose you're expecting a love story here. Maybe

some great change she made in my life that pulled me from the blade and the gun. Sorry to disappoint. Just solid love and good sense. Sometimes that's all you need. Two boys. A little piece of land I bought with the money she'd made me start saving. The promise of more. Until that damn cough.

I took another swallow, rubbed my eyes. The wind was getting feisty outside, blowing in the breaks between logs. I lit a fire in the hearth, stoked it a little, and settled back. She knew about my past. Made me tell her, if you can imagine that. Told me no secret was worth the poison it brought into a relationship. So I laid myself bare. I couldn't tell you why then, and I couldn't tell you why now. But I can tell you it was important. I'd never been one for priests and their absolution. But here was a woman willing to hear, to eat the sins of my past.

So I shared. And she listened. And when I finished, she gave me a look like a man weighing a prospector's gold. Didn't say a word for five minutes, and when she did, it was "I forgive you." And again, I don't know why, but I accepted that. If this woman who'd known shit all about me before could forgive my every vile sin, maybe I could find a way to live with them, too.

One more pull on the bottle. I watched the fire dance. Orange and red, orange and red. It reminded me of past fires. The world drifted, shifted.

Someone was shouting. Kent? He grabbed my shoulder, pulled me behind a chunk of masonry that'd fallen off the keep. The air was filled with cordite and the clash of steel. Somewhere ahead, Rangers clashed with Henrik's Hawks, though you couldn't see shit for the smoke. The ringing in my ears subsided, and Kent's voice hammered into my head.

"You listening?" He shouted.

"What?" I blinked, worked a finger in my ear.

Felt like they'd been plugged. No one expected the keg to blow the way it had. Must've taken half the wall down. Men screamed from under the rubble, adding to the noise.

"Said they're occupied in the courtyard. You want that money, we're gonna have to go around."

"Yeah, yeah," I said.

Checked my pistol. The charges were still dry in their chambers, the balls packed down. Checked the knives on my hips. Still in their sheathes. Nodded to Kent. Blue lightning cracked in the courtyard, throwing men and dirt into the air.

"Fuck," he muttered. Black skin crinkled around his eyes. "They got a Caller."

"Ain't nothin' to be done about it. I null him here, he'll see us. Let's go," I said.

Kent led, long rifle slung across his back, blade at his side. I followed, pistol in one hand, knife in the other. We picked our way over busted chunks of wall. Someone spotted us, called out. I turned, saw a man with his legs under a piece of fallen rock. Cut his throat. He twitched once, lay still and quiet.

"That necessary?" Kent asked.

"Might've drawn someone to us."

Kent grunted, and we slipped through the breach and hugged the wall, sidling toward the keep. The noise was louder here, the chaos nearer. Men died and gave death back a few hundred yards away. A man in white enameled armor etched with sigils raised his hand, and another bolt of lightning struck the center of the Hawks' lines. They were starting to give up the fight. I cursed.

"What is it?" Kent asked.

I hunkered down behind an abandoned wagon.

"That damn Caller. Rangers are going to have this in hand, and then we're out a payday." I thought for a minute. "Hand me that rifle."

"What've you got planned?"

"Just give me the damned rifle."

He handed the long gun over, and I checked the cylinder. Five shots. I sighted down the barrel. The fight was winding down, and the Rangers had already clapped irons on a few men. I drew a bead on the Caller, standing to the side, a smug look on his face. I erased it with a lead ball.

"Nice shot," Kent said.

I grunted and fired four more times, taking the throat out of a Ranger, another in the chest, and two Hawks in the leg and stomach. *Bang bang BANG BANG*

I started in my chair. Someone hammered on the cabin door, heavy blows like a smith at the forge. I looked around blearily.

"Wil! Wil! Open up! I ain't gonna stand in this blasted cold all night!"

I stumbled to the door, fumbled the latch. The door shivered again.

"Hold on, ya impatient bastard," I muttered.

I got the latch undid, threw the door open. Kent stood there, Black as ever, shivering, silver hair bright in the moonlight.

"Come in, then," I said. "Letting the warm out."

He stepped in and hung his cloak while I closed the door.

"Take a seat," I said.

I scooped up the bottle of whiskey. He looked about ready to sit in Ginny's chair.

"Not there," I said. "Kitchen."

We walked into the mean kitchen with its crooked cabinets and cracked washbasin. I dug out two tumblers and placed them on the table, then poured us each a measure of the liquor. We sat in silence for a minute, sipping at the whiskey, letting its fire warm us. My head cleared a little.

"Heard about Ginny," Kent said.

"Aye. Made the trip all the way down here for that?" I asked.

He fidgeted with his glass, shot a furtive glance off toward the boys' room.

"How're things?" He asked.

"Tight," I said.

It was true. I hadn't the heart to tell Ginny the last of our money was drying up. The crops weren't bringing in enough, and the school had let her go. I wasn't going to be able to feed the boys next season, let alone clothe or keep them in medicine if they needed it. I thought about the way she'd made me donate the money I'd taken from the Henrik job, and a barb of spite pricked me. I slugged away the last of my glass and poured more.

"Yeah," Kent said. "What I thought."

"What's that mean?"

"Means you were good with a blade, better with a gun, but shit with a plow."

I shrugged. He wasn't wrong.

"What'd you come for?" I asked.

"Told you, heard about Ginny."

I snorted. "Kent, you ain't told me a truth I haven't had to drag out of you a day in your life. And I'm too damn old, tired, and drunk to struggle right now. So, tell me why you're here, or I'm gonna toss your ass back into the cold, and you can ride on back to your woman and your cattle."

He sighed, turned the glass round in his hands. "Heard tell of a bounty."

"So?"

I didn't see what that had to do with me. Unless it was on me. I eyed the old pistol hung beside the cabinets, the dusty holster. It wasn't nothing but dead iron yet. Hadn't been loaded or oiled in years. I might get the drop on him if I could make it to the butcher block where Ginny kept the knives. But I doubted it.

Kent seemed to know what I was thinking.

"Relax. Not on you," he scoffed. "Ornery old bastard. Bunch of boys came up to Copper Creek. Roughed up some of the girls."

I shook my head. "I got boys of my own. Besides, you know I ain't done shit but plow and plow for years."

"Maybe." Kent drained his glass. "But you could use the cash. How old are those boys, anyway?"

"Twelve," I said.

I chose to ignore the other comment. It stung. Nothing reminds a man that he's failing more than someone commenting on his poor provisional skills, and I wasn't the sort of man to let barbs go once I picked at them. *Hadn't* been. Ginny'd knocked that out of me.

"Old enough, then," Kent said. "Tika could swing by and check on 'em once a week. Ain't so far to ride."

I thought about it. I did need the money. I didn't see why Kent needed me.

"Why you coming to me with this?" I asked.

"Maybe I figure I owe you something. Maybe because those boys don't deserve to get sick or cold or turned out when you can't make your taxes. Maybe because when you see an old horse, you look at it and think of how it used to run, and you just want to see it run one more time. But mostly because you were the meanest sonovabitch I'd ever known. And smart, too. If anyone can find those boys, and get us paid, I'd trust you to do it."

I poured another glass of whiskey. Shook the empty bottle and set it on the table. The man made a lot of sense. In the old days, sense was a thing I'd reserve for those too cautious to live, too timid to fight. Now though... he was right. I had a responsibility. I had a promise to keep to my wife. I slugged the glass down, felt the fire in my guts kindle for a moment. I looked hard at Kent.

"All right, then. You can bunk down on the floor. Some blankets in that cabinet. I'll tell the boys in the morning, and we'll go."

Kent smiled. "Made a good choice, Wil."

I narrowed my eyes, set my mouth. "That remains to be seen."

He chuckled and set to making his bed. I stayed up a little longer, watching the fire, wondering if this would be the sort of thing Ginny would approve. Funny thing about judging another's thoughts. Hard enough when they're alive. Damn near impossible when they're in the ground. But I decided that in this, she'd likely give me a little rein. And if she wouldn't, what would she say from under the prairie?

Two

It was raining bullets, the light cold-filtered through gray clouds when the boys followed me to the yard. Kent was already waiting, horse saddled, that old long gun of his in a leather holster covering the works and keeping the powder dry. I eyed it, felt the weight of my own pistol under my long coat. I'd been up before dawn, rubbing the rust off and oiling the cylinder until it clicked smoothly when spun.

I turned to the boys, squatted til my coat trailed in the mud.

"Y'all keep the house. Shouldn't be gone more than a week, maybe two. Mind Tika when she comes 'round." I turned to Fallon. "Don't let the crops go fallow. You bring 'em in when they're ready."

He nodded, turned back to the house, disappeared inside. I looked to Carter. "You mind your brother. I need you to keep an eye out. He's a soft soul, that one, whether he lets on or no."

"Aren't you gonna leave me iron, papa?" He asked.

I shook my head. "My big knife's in the closet. Don't pull it unless you mean to use it. And there's a good bow in my room. Same thing. You need anything, I want you to saddle up your ma's horse and take her down to see Tika. The two of you can share the saddle. You ain't too big yet. But I don't anticipate trouble. Been a while since the Rangers or the Hawks been around."

He nodded, wiped his eyes. Rain rolled off the end of his nose. Maybe it was tears, but I wasn't about to shame him pointing it out. That'd just leave both of us feeling bad. Absence turns feelings like that into abscesses, sore festering pits of resentment no amount of cutting can heal.

"Go on now, get inside. Can't have you getting sick."

Carter turned, ran in through the rain. I watched the door close, then turned to Kent.

"Give me a minute."

He nodded, and I made my way over to Ginny's grave. I stood over it, hat in hand. The rain had made a muddy slop of the earth, and I thought of her down there, drowning. I pushed the image away and wiped the rain from my face. A futile gesture, but what isn't in this world at times?

"I'm goin' away for a bit. Keep an eye on the boys. I know you wouldn't approve of what I'm doing, but it's for the better of our family." I looked up, rain falling into my eyes, tilted my head down again, took a breath. "That at least, I know you'd approve of. I love you."

I put my hat on and walked back to Kent, then climbed into Drafter's saddle. He was an old horse, little more than a mule these days, but sturdy and steady. It'd been a while since I'd rode in earnest, and I'd need a solid set of feet under me. I reined him around and clicked once, the old pony kicking into a trot. Kent joined me.

We rode in silence, the creak of leather and jingle of harness the only sounds aside from the steady patter of rain. Eventually, the track curved away from the house and down a hill. I didn't look back.

We were a few miles down the road when Kent finally spoke up.

"They'll be okay, Wil," he said. "That Carter's got a good head on him."

"I know that," I said.

"He'll take care of Fallon. And you know Tika'll look in on 'em."

"I know."

"It's not like we're riding off to war, you know."

"I know."

"Then why you got that hangdog expression on your face?"

"Do I? Just thought that was my face."

Silence for a time. Rain dripped off the brim of my hat, made tapping sounds against the oilskin at my shoulders. It carried a chill, but the heat from Drafter funneled up the inside of the coat and kept me warm.

"Where to?" I asked.

"Copper Creek. Got to get a bounty chit from the girls up there."

The prairie passed by, from the rich loam of the river valley to gently rolling hills pockmarked by past conflict. Flashes of it splashed my memory. Ten thousand screaming men. Gunsmoke so thick you could part it with a knife. The wet splatter of a bullet smashing through flesh and bone. The hard tearing of a blade through skin and organ. The pound of feet. Cannonfire. Screaming bolts of lighting, airships dropping men into the field and tearing away again or detonating as some lucky bastard found the engine. Fire, acid, choking mist.

I blinked, the ribs of an airship, long covered with sod and lichen jutted from the ground. Ivy wrapped around the struts and bright pink flowers the size of my fingernail bloomed there. A crater filled with rainwater. The skeleton of some horror the Nulls had brought into being. Ghosts at the edge of my vision. I shook it off.

"How long?" I asked Kent.

"Hm? Oh, 'bout a week, like you told the boys. Two days to Copper Creek, a night there. Two days to find the bounty and back, then another two days home."

"How much?"

"Hundred each."

That didn't feel right. "Hundred *each*? Where'd whores get that kind of money?"

"You care? They're whores, Wil. Where you think they got that kind of money?"

"Hm." Hundred was a lot of money. I might even be able to buy a house in one of the cities west of the prairie, set the boys up with a teacher. "Might be I took up the wrong kind of work."

"You're too ugly to whore."

"Aye."

"Then, what?" Kent asked.

"Boys need schoolin', now their mother's gone," I said.

"You could teach them."

I looked at him. "I don't want to teach them what I know. It's bad enough I had to show Carter bow and knife."

He raised an eyebrow. "No?"

"No." I spat on the trail. "Boys ought to know more than killin' and carousin'."

"Never hurt us."

"Yeah, not us."

He didn't ask what I meant. I didn't volunteer. I still felt Ginny's loss, sharper than the blade I'd left at home, her lessons still heavier than stone. She'd done her best to drill some civility into me and the boys, some semblance of respectability. If it didn't wholly take, it wasn't her fault. Men are savage creatures, as wont to turn to anger and violence as any animal. Sure, you could dress them up, give them a bit of book learnin', but in the end, they were all terror and blood and hate. Least in my experience.

The sound of water accompanied us as we rode deeper into the plain. A creek the color of dirty metal swelled its banks to our right. Still thin, nothing the horses couldn't cross. Drafter plodded along, and I let the burbling of the stream and my horse's hooves squelching in mud quiet my mind.

The rain let up just as the sun slipped the horizon, a dog loose of its leash. We found a stand of sycamore trees and bedded under them, a small fire and a brace of rabbit our comfort. It'd been a long ride, and we were both sore and soaked. I lay in my bedroll looking up to stars that had crept from behind retreating clouds.

"You remember Fletcher?" Kent asked.

"That skinny little fucker outta Coldharbor?" I asked.

"Yeah, you remember the way he'd hitch up his pants every time he tried to act tough?"

I barked out a laugh. "Right up until that sergeant—was it Naughton?—cut his belt. There he is, standing in the street, trying to threaten the man, and flapping in the wind."

"Flapping's generous," Kent said.

I snorted. "Ass like a board. Whatever happened to him?"

"Sheriff got him over in Redhook. Took him up to the Church."

"Ah, fuckin' shame. He was always good for a laugh."

Kent chuckled softly. "Yeah."

We listened to water dripping from the branches of the little copse. Something small scurried through the brush. A pheasant called out.

"Ain't they got a sheriff up there? Copper Creek, I mean," I said.

"Yeah, what's your point?" Kent asked.

"Seems like this is sheriff work."

"You gone soft, Wil?"

"No, I just don't want to get into it with the law. Look where it got Fletcher."

Kent scoffed, gave a sudden guffaw. "You, worried about some tin-star?"

"Ginny always said they was just trying to do their job. Said I should be ashamed of the ones I killed. They had family, you know."

"Yeah, so did we."

He let it drop for a few minutes. I thought about the

Church's pogroms, the lists and the punishments. My pa had died before it started, but my mother wasn't so lucky. Kent's folks, too. They'd carted them off by train to the camps. 'Reeducation', they called it. Wasn't nothing more than indoctrination, and failing that, shifts in the mines 'til you dropped.

Somewhere on the plain, a coyote howled, and another answered its call. I knew what they were feeling. That loneliness creeps up. Makes you need someone to howl with. A twig snapped in the fire.

"You losing your guts already?" Kent asked.

"Why would you ask a thing like that?" I snapped. I pushed down a rising tide of anger.

"Seems you're holding Ginny awful close. Like you're afraid of rilin' the dead."

The rage pushed past the block I'd set, spilled over. I clenched my jaw, stopped myself from reaching for my pistol. He couldn't know. Not entirely. He still had Tika.

"You want to shut up now."

"Yeah, maybe I do. Night, Wil."

I didn't answer. Let the fire burn down before I closed my eyes, and still saw Ginny in the flames in the dark.

Morning was full of fog on the plain, dew on the grass, and the crack of gunfire echoing off the trees. I missed, cursed, and reloaded.

"What in the everloving fuck are you up to?" Kent asked from behind me.

I fired off another round at a can I'd set up on a log. Missed again.

"Practice. You know the last time I fired this thing?"

The pistol kicked, knocked a chunk of bark off a nearby tree.

"Was it Higgstown?"

Another kick, another miss.

"Might've been."

"Shit, that was what..."

I fired my last round, kicked up a clot of dirt three feet to the side. I holstered the pistol and concentrated, forcing my will into a still point in my chest. It came hard, like swimming through mud, but finally I found my focus. I rolled up my sleeves, the tattoos there already glowing. I opened a small gate through the Empyrean and found the stuff that made up the can, a small ball of energy marking its place in reality, and crushed it in my fists. The can imploded, and the portal winked out.

"About twenty years," I said.

Wisps of smoke curled from my hands. I walked back to camp and sat on a stump. Started to reload the pistol. Charge, ball, tamp, grease, cap. Charge, ball, tamp, grease, cap. Slow, but necessary to keep each from overfiring. Kent watched me for three cylinders, then spoke up.

"When's the last time you played with that demon shit?"

"It ain't demon shit. It just ain't what the Church or their Callers approve of."

"Uh huh."

Loaded another cylinder.

"You heard about Roper?" He asked.

I knew what he was getting at. We'd all heard about Roper. About how he'd opened a path to the Empyrean and something came through. Strung his guts across a mile of field.

"He was sloppy. You don't open the really big portals by yourself. Not ever."

"Yeah? You ever open one?"

Shook my head. I had. Didn't like to talk about it. Wasn't his business. I hadn't even told Ginny. She was a good Church girl. Would've had my skin at the least. I suspect more though, that she would have left, and I couldn't have that. A man tastes sweetwater after a lifetime of drinking from a swamp, it wakes something in him.

"Yeah, okay," Kent said.

I finished loading the pistol, slipped it back onto my hip. The day had dried out, and though it still held a chill, at least it wasn't wet.

"Should get going. Not gonna make any money sitting around jawing," I said.

Kent nodded, and we saddled up, kicking the horses into an easy trot.

The copse of ash trees fell away as we rode, and before long, tall grasses sprung up in the vales between the hills. Somewhere to the right, the creek had widened and now chuckled and babbled cheerfully over smooth stone. Cattails clicked in the wind. I thought that at another time, I could enjoy this ride. As it was, a kernel of doubt dug at me, like a burr in a boot.

I thought about the boys, alone in the house, and if they'd be there when I got back. About what Ginny might say about my running off to do violence. I worried about the fact I couldn't hit a godsdamned can from three meters. I worried that the Empyrean had come so readily, even though I hadn't touched it since the Pit. Mostly, I wondered if Kent was right in a way, and I was playing with things I shouldn't.

I looked over at him. Still an edge to the old man, his head on swivel. His hand rested easily on the butt of his rifle, the other holding the reins loose. Tika hadn't tamed him. Or maybe she'd given up. A scar crossed the back of his neck to just up under his ear. I remembered how he'd got that.

The Pit. Forty feet below the surface. Each tier a ring surrounded by a spiral ramp with no way out aside from through twenty armed men. The worst of the worst. We'd been down there six months, carved out a niche for ourselves. Kent could get a man what he needed, I could hurt a man when that was the thing they were looking for.

Until Kruger. Big bastard, tattooed from neck to waist. They said he'd had his division burn an entire village and everyone in it to the ground. The man made enemies fast, and before long, the other inmates had come to Kent and I. Kent had taken the contract, which got him the scar.

The big man came for us in the middle of the night. He'd got wind somehow of the plan to do him in—no shortage of snitches inside—and came for us alone. Cocky bastard. He kicked in our doors, dragging Kent out first.

Kruger cut him from behind, then opened a gate while my partner bled. What came through was seven foot and covered in armor the color of dried blood. It ripped Kruger's head off, and I worked on instinct. Opened a gate of my own and let the demons out.

I don't know what happened after. Best I can piece together is that there was a fight between the two hellish beasts. Tore each other apart.

Kent won't fully say, even now. Some things scar a man and recalling them's like picking a scab.

That's when he reckoned I turned mean. Whatever the

case, a merc band came recruiting and bought our way out two weeks later. Normally, we would've rotted there for the rest of our lives. I think after the dustup on the tiers, the Church was just happy to see the backside of us. As for the inmates, I don't think I've ever seen a group of hardasses so happy to see someone go.

"Hey," Kent said. "Woolgathering?"

I blinked away the memory. Looked at the sun. It had crept past noon. I must've been down a while.

"Yeah, sorry."

He jerked his head to the side. "I think we're being followed."

"How many?"

"Just one. And noisy as fuck, too."

"On foot?"

"Yeah. Trying to hide in the grass."

"You go on ahead like you ain't seen a thing. I'll circle back."

He nodded, and I spurred the horse around the next hill, dropping into the valley. I stopped Drafter on the lee side, and dismounted, then crept through the grasses. The trail was plain as day. Crushed stalks, footprints in the mud. I followed for a few yards, then caught a rustle ahead. I crouched, creeping between the stalks of burred wheat, legs and back aching from the ride.

My quarry was just a few feet ahead. Slim thing, white shirt, dun trousers. A pistol on her hip. A rawhide strap held her hair back. I eased closer, stuck my pistol in her back. She stiffened, raising her hands.

"Good," I said. "That's smart. Keep your hands away, and you'll live. Who sent you?"

"No one," she said. Her voice was a light tenor, pleasant, but taut with nerves.

"You ain't with the law?"

"No sir."

"Mean to bushwhack us?"

"No sir."

"Then there ain't many reasons to follow two men across the prairie. What is it you're after?"

"I wanted to join up."

"With?"

"With you. You and the black man up there."

"And just who are we?"

She turned, a smile on her face. She was pretty, but young. I might've found her interesting twenty years ago. Now I just felt annoyed.

"You're Wil Cutter, sir. And that's Black Kent. And you're going after a bounty."

Kent had rode up while she was talking, and sat easy in his saddle, the rifle out of its holster and across his lap.

"Should I shoot her, Wil?" He asked.

I shook my head. "Nah. Unless she doesn't go home. Then maybe we have to."

"What's she after?"

"Says she wants to join up."

"I do," she said.

"Why would we want that?" I asked. "Split the money three ways instead of two?"

"Because you can't hit the broad side of a barn with a brick," she said.

Kent snorted and I shot him a look. He stifled it, and I looked back at the girl.

"I can shoot just fine."

"Yeah, maybe from you to me."

Kent laughed at that, and I put the gun away. He'd blown the threat all to hell anyway. She lowered her hands.

"Okay, and you can do better?"

"Bet your ass," she said.

I walked back to my horse, saddled up. Looked at Kent, then back at her.

"Wouldn't be the worst thing," Kent said. "We don't know how many of those boys there are."

It was true, after all. And even a third of the money would be enough to take care of my boys til they were men. Still, I had to get a dig in.

"You got a name?" I asked.

"Anne," she said. "Bloody Anne. Kilt more men at eighteen than you did by thirty."

"Mmhm. You got a horse, killer?"

She lifted her chin. "Left him over yonder."

"All right. Get your horse and catch up."

She ran off, and Kent and I made our way back to the trail.

"She'll be a help," Kent said.

I pinched the bridge of my nose. "I sure as hell hope so. Otherwise, we just invited someone else to die with us."

"That's the Wil I know. Morbid as fuck."

I grinned at him, and we rode on.

Three

Anne caught up just as the trail started to curve toward the creek again. The sun rode high, and in the distance, a smudge on the horizon that had to be Copper Creek. I looked over.

"You ride well," I said.

"Aye, and I do other things well," she said.

"You gonna be a smart mouth the whole way?"

"Why? Yours lose its wit?"

"Gods save me. Kent, ride over here."

"Why?" he asked.

"So I don't shoot her."

"I think we already established you couldn't hit me," she said.

I spurred my horse the other side of Kent and we rode in silence for a while.

"See that hawk?" She asked.

Kent and I looked up. I spotted it wheeling above us, a brown speck against the blue.

"Yeah? So?" Kent said.

"Bet I could hit it."

"Waste of bullets," I said. "You gonna eat it if you do?"

"What?"

"Shouldn't shoot anything you don't intend to kill that ain't a man unless you intend to eat it or you're in danger."

"I think you're just scared."

"Scared you're gonna drive me over the edge."

"Now, hold on, there, girl," Kent said. "I ain't never seen Wil scared of a fucking thing."

"I think he's scared he'd lose that bet."

I sighed. I knew she wasn't going to let up trying to make her bones unless I gave a little.

"Go on, then. First one to down it wins."

"Yeah, what do I win?"

"You can have my share of the bounty."

"Hot damn."

"But if I win, you keep your trap shut til the Creek."

"Deal, old man. Who goes first?"

"Have at it," I said.

"Wil…" Kent said. I raised a hand.

"Let her try," I said.

She whipped her pistol free with surprising speed, snapping off a shot. The hawk continued to soar above.

"My turn," I said.

I opened a gate and snatched the life from the bird through the Empyrean. It plummeted, crashing into the earth somewhere further afield. Anne slipped her pistol into its holster, mouth working silently. Kent started to laugh, his whole frame shaking.

"You cheated!" She said.

I shrugged. "Only rule was to drop it. Now... shush."

She clamped her lips shut, and to her credit, kept her part of the deal.

The trail widened as we approached Copper Creek. It had once been a company town, big on mining. Now, it was little more than a waypoint where the water ran brown and the people trudged out gray lives. The outskirts were shanties and abandoned mining housing, roofs and porches sagging. Laundry hung on lines strung between the homes like sagging cobwebs. Men and women sat on their porches in the afternoon heat, shooing flies or sipping tea from dirty glasses. None made eye contact as we rode in.

Kent drew his horse close to mine, leaned in. Anne sat her horse off to the side, looking down on the town.

"These people look spooked," Kent said.

The road curved, taking us into the town proper. The buildings here were better maintained, though their facades were faded. Company store, hotel, saloon. A milliner and tailor, a tack store and stables, boarding houses. Nestled between the hotel and the saloon was a two-story house, floral curtains in the windows, women—clean and scantily clad—lounging on the porch. That was our destination.

Anne reined her horse in that direction, and I stopped her with a hiss.

"What? You afraid of some ladies?" She asked.

I shook my head. "No need to be obvious. Law might be looking for bounty hunters. Might want to shut them down."

She looked to Kent, who nodded, then back to me. Shrugged and spat in the dirt.

"I'm just a girl looking for a good time. Why don't you old-timers go have a drink? No need to wear yourselves out."

I saw the look in her eye, the same one Ginny got when she had something in her head she wasn't about to let go. I nodded, and spurred Drafter toward the saloon. Kent followed close.

"Think she'll kick up trouble?" He asked.

I glance back, to where she was hitching the horse and greeting the women. Looked ahead again.

"No idea. If she does, we don't know her."

"That's cold, Wil."

"Is what it is. Horny's one thing. Got no truck with stupid."

We reined in before the saloon and hitched the horses. It'd been a couple days, so I fixed a feedbag and brushed Drafter while Kent went inside. I was working the knots out of his mane when a stout man, followed by three more, climbed the stairs, bootheels echoing on the wood. They pushed into the saloon, and I waited. I'd seen the blue tattoos on the man's arm, and the badge on his chest. The law here was a Caller.

Voices from inside carried on the still air.

"You ain't from town, are ya?" One voice asked.

Another, "Looks like a Rebel boy to me."

I put the comb away and climbed the steps myself, pushing the swinging doors open. The bar stank of beer and unwashed men. The Caller and his goons had surrounded Kent, where he sat alone at a table.

"Ain't a bounty hunter, are you?" Asked the Caller.

I pushed past them and took a seat beside Kent, leaning back so my hand and gun were free. The man who'd cornered Kent had a broad, tanned face, wrinkles around the eyes and climbing his forehead. He wore his clothes and gun easy and stood like he was used to violence. Probably a veteran then. Just one who'd been on the right—the winning—side.

"Sorry, didn't catch your name," I said.

"Dag. Dag Hunter."

He said it like he expected a reaction. I looked over at Kent, who shrugged.

"I know it." The man who spoke up was thin as a whip, with a nose like a hook. Long white hair hung from under his hat. He wore a three-piece suit, a pair of pistols crossed over his hips. He leaned against the bar, easy as a willow in the wind.

"From down around Henrik, right? You were there when the rebels surrendered. Heard you killed fifteen yourself."

A sound of thunder. Guns and cordite. Hawks and Rangers dying in equal measure. Kent and I had only come for the rumored gold the noble there was hoarding. What we found was a travesty. Anger welled up in me, and I had to push it down and away.

Dag shook his head. "It was ten. And I was there before the surrender. Took a bullet in the leg. They had to cart me off. And you, where were you, Ben?"

"Why, I was in Enla, of course. We don't truck with rebels or the violence they bring. That's what's wrong with your country, if you ask me. Not enough respect for leadership. No one dares rebel against a king or an empress. But a Church—that's just begging for a fight. Men should be free to worship as they please. It just so happens that kings are real. Your god? Well..."

I watched Dag's hand drift to his pistol. He stood a little cocked to compensate for his knee, but the man was still solid, and his eyes clear. I put ten to one he'd shoot Ben down before the other man whipped even one of his guns out.

"You want to go back to drinking, Ben," Dag said.

"This swill? No thanks," Ben said, and threw a couple coins on the counter.

He made his way out of the saloon, bumping shoulders with a couple of Dag's men on the way. They turned back to Kent and I. Dag sized us up for another minute.

"Don't know why you're here. Don't much care. But I don't tolerate bounty seekers or anyone else looking to subvert the law."

His eyes narrowed at the markings on my wrists.

"And I certainly don't love a Null. You boys keep your noses clean for the night, and hit the trail tomorrow, and we won't have a problem."

He turned to go, and two of his men took seats at a table across from Kent and me. The saloon doors swung in his passage, splitting the beam of sunlight as it passed through. The bartender wended between the tables and took our order. I'd had little else but rabbit and dried meat on the trail and looked forward to a steak, maybe a couple potatoes. When he was gone, Kent leaned in.

"What're we gonna do now?"

I took a sip of the bartender's whiskey. It wasn't bad, if a little watered down.

"Go after the bounty."

"I thought you didn't want to cross the law."

I thought about it. I didn't. But knowing this man was there, slaughtering rebels at Henrik, dug up something I'd thought buried. I felt a bit of the old mean streak slip back in.

"Changed my mind."

He gave me a long, level look. "Okay, then. I'll get us rooms."

"Get one for the girl, too. Assuming she can walk after all the whorin'."

He nodded and set off. I sat and drank, time pushing memory at me like sand before a hot wind.

The breach at Vint. Five thousand bodies roaring into a hole in the wall like blood and pus crossing a wound in flesh. Some, too weak to hold a blade, cholera from the siege leaking into the water, shit running down the backs of wasted thighs, them falling, not getting up, coughing blood and phlegm into the filth. Ballistae hammering the walls, shattering them, fire raining from the Callers, melting stone and brick like tallow, men made into flesh candles before collapsing into rendered fat and blackened bone. The stink. And in the middle, men with severed limbs, broken limbs, snapped back white bone limbs and exposed cheeks and teeth, eyes dangling, red ruin in the flames. Some still crawled, forward to the city nearby. What was nearby? A mile? A thousand? Quiet overgrown towers teeming with moss and vine and bodies in the streets, in the hovels, in the mansions and palaces and plazas. Tired dead bodies lying on the stones, and I would not be one.

The sound of saloon doors snapping open, and I was back in my chair.

Anne stumbled in, flushed and grinning. She sauntered over to my table.

"Lookin' melancholy as hell, old man."

"Looking like you got friction burns on your flaps. You find out what we needed?"

"Yeah, we going right away?"

"In the morning. Head on up. Kent got you a room."

"You gonna sit here and cry into your whiskey?"

"I'm gonna sit here and think. You should try it sometime."

She muttered something about shriveled balls and made her way up the wide staircase. The shadows were lengthening in the room, and I paid the bartender for the rest of the bottle. Memories slipped from the shadows again, smothered me.

"No, not like—not like that. You got to ease it back," I said.

Carter was eight, but old enough to hold the pistol if he braced it with his free hand. He sighed and took his thumb off the hammer, letting it click back into place. I cringed just a little.

"You can't let it snap back like that, either. Too much, and it'll ignite the cap. Then you got a misfire."

"Sorry, pa."

"Don't be sorry, just do it—" I took a breath. Almost said 'do it right', but that's what my old man would've said to me. And there was no love lost there. "Just be careful," I amended.

He nodded, and took a breath, eased the hammer back.

"Good. Now let it out, and squeeze. Don't pull. You pull, and you'll jerk your shot wide."

He did as told. The big gun kicked in his hands, and while the barrel popped up, the shot hit the melon I'd set in the yard, punching a hole clean through.

"Good. Good work."

I took the pistol from him, holstered it, then hunkered down.

"What's the rule?" I asked.

"We don't point at nothin' we ain't gonna shoot."

"Good. Now get inside."

He scampered off, and I turned to watch him go. Ginny stood in the door with a small smile.

"You're good with him."

"I try. Just wish I had more to teach the boy."

She walked over, looped her arms around my waist, looked up into my eyes. "That's why I'm here. You teach him the stuff you know; I teach him what I do, and we might make a whole man of him."

"You saying I ain't a whole man?"

"I'm saying you weren't 'til you met me."

I grinned. "Clever. You think you're clever."

She returned the smile. "I *know* I'm clever, Wil Cutter. Taught you, didn't I?"

"And a wiseacre."

"And here I was just about to ask you to teach me what you know."

"I rescind my comment, madam. I meant to say wise beyond your years."

"Shut up and kiss me, you idiot."

I did, the sun setting at our backs, the smell of trail dust and summer wheat in the air.

They came for us when I was in my cups. There wasn't a struggle to speak of—one minute I was dozing at the table, the next they'd taken my gun and dragged the three of us—me, Kent, and Anne into the street. They took to kicking the shit out of us in short order. I curled up, but still felt a couple ribs break, my wrist wrench. Kent got the worst of it, Dag's goons beating him unconscious. Anne managed to struggle up, run into a nearby boarding house. Dag sent two men after her. They dragged her back, kicking and screaming, and he pistol-whipped her quiet.

I was lucky. As lucky as a man can get in that sort of situation. The whiskey dulled the worst of the pain. But inside, I felt that cold pit of rage building. The men parted, and Dag leaned in.

"The only reason I ain't hanging the lot of you is I need a lesson for the others. I've had men in here hunting that bounty for a week now, and they're shitting up this town. Ain't their place. Ain't your place. You tell the others to stay away, or next time they—or you—show your face here, you'll swing. Get me?"

Then they knocked me on the head, too, and the world when white, then black.

Four

Farson had promised us something back then.

He'd come out of the east, a Cleric fed up with the Church.

The world was moving on, he said, and the Church was determined to clutch power for as long as possible. At our expense, naturally. Tyranny is always the last gasp of the old guard. And Farson had promised more. Freedom. Equality. Enough food for our bellies and roofs over our heads.

So, we fought. And we lost. But not before we burned it all. Now there was neither Church nor rebel, but remnants of both who remembered old hatreds.

I swam in fitful memory for a time. Past atrocities. Murder in the night as the enemy slept. Poisoned wells. Women and children under the axe. Not all mine, but I certainly owned my share. Then I remembered the peace brought by a good woman. The pride in raising children. And as those things passed away, relegated to later concerns, only one pushed its way to the surface. I wanted payback.

And I wanted that payday. Maybe for family, but the more indignities the world heaped on me, more to prove a point.

Don't fuck with me and mine.

That's why I didn't believe for a second the attack from Dag came as any ideal to uphold the law. He'd seen my tattoos, and I his. I'd let him be. He couldn't do the same. And now I was waking up with the sort of unique pain only the absence of whiskey and a beating the night before could conjure.

I groaned and opened my eyes to a pair of light brown ones decorated with a spate of freckles across the eyelids. Her hair was the color of sunrise. Fresh scars, the flesh still raw pink, ran from under her jaw to her temple. They should've been raw, which meant a healer'd been at her, at least.

"Those boys do that to you?" I asked.

She nodded.

"Where are they?"

She pressed a poultice against my ribs. They were the color of an oil spill. I hissed in pain as she used a wrap to hold it in place.

"None of yours," she said. "We withdrew the bounty."

"Yeah? Maybe I got personal reasons now." I managed to raise my head enough to look around.

Kent lay prone on a bench against the wall. Anne was nowhere to be seen.

"Where's the girl?"

"Outside. Puking her guts out."

I nodded at Kent. "He woke yet?"

She shook her head, ran a wet cloth over the worst of the dried blood on my face.

"You're gonna let us get beat to shit for nothing, then?"

"No one asked you to come," she said. A defensive edge crept into her voice.

"Hundred is more than ask enough. You know that."

"Because I'm a whore? You even know I got a name?" She threw the cloth at me. I caught it.

"Because you ain't stupid. What's your name?"

"Cora."

"Where are those boys, Cora?"

"I can't guarantee you any money."

"I reckon they might have some of their own," I said.

She bit her lip. The door opened, and Anne staggered in, looking six shades of green. For a moment, the scarred woman glanced between the two of us. She came to a decision.

"Hennick's boys. Ranch is about two days west from here."

I thought about it. Tika would have to make do. The boys would be okay. Winter was close, but not on us, yet. I looked up at Anne.

"You coming?"

"I ain't got no damn gun."

Cora looked apprehensive once more. She reached under my bench and pulled out a canvas bundle, unwrapped it. Two pistols, new. A box of something I hadn't seen before. Anne whistled, and I winced at the sound.

"These are the new ones. How'd you get these?" She asked.

"Boy who cut me up left them behind," Cora said. "Probably thought it was restitution. Maybe he was just scared of the consequences and didn't want to get caught out."

"Well, shit. He was rich after all," I said.

I picked up the pistol, weighed it. It felt good in my hand. I dug a few shells—that's what Cora called them—out of the box and slipped them into the cylinders. Anne was doing the same with the matching gun. I pulled my shirt on, covering the scars and tattoos crossing my body, then slipped the pistol into my holster. I nodded over at Kent.

"You take care of him. If he wakes up, you send him to me."

She nodded, and I stood. Swayed a little and grabbed the wall for support.

"You gonna make it?" Anne asked.

"I'll be fine, greenguts."

"You heard me?"

"They heard you in Elan."

"Shit."

I steadied myself and walked to the door.

"If we ain't back in two days, you send Kent home. I got boys that need minding."

Cora nodded, and I left, Anne at my heels. Our horses were tethered to a post outside the old mining outbuilding. Copper Creek stood a half mile away. Dag hadn't gone to a lot of trouble to move us out. Hadn't even set a guard. Cocky bastard. I unhitched Drafter. It took me three tries to get into the saddle, and I vomited a thin stream of bile once up there. My ribs screamed. I looked over to the kid.

"You got anything in that pack of yours?"

She rummaged around, came up with a bottle of rotgut. I snatched it from her, took a long swallow. When the fire faded, so did some of the pain. I corked it and set it into my own bags.

"Hey, that's..."

"Necessary," I said.

I spurred Drafter onto the trail and we rode for the Hennick ranch.

The road from Copper Creek dwindled into a pair of wagon ruts before long. The landscape turned sere brown, sagebrush and buttes vying for attention. We'd only been riding west for the better part of a day, but the chill of the morning had already lessened, and the earth threatened to turn to parched desert. The effects of so much magic lashed into the world at the violent whims of men.

Anne kept up, quieter than her usual self. Maybe that beating from Dag's boys in the Creek knocked some sense into her. I shook my head. That wasn't right. Wasn't a beating I took in my life made me wiser. Just meaner.

I recalled my first, at the hands of my old man. He'd caught me out whorin' with the Thomas' daughter when I should've been stacking hay. Whipped me bloody with a willow branch. I could barely sit for two days after.

The old man had no compunction about whipping me for the slightest infraction. And if it wasn't the switch, it was his wide old leather belt. And if it wasn't that, his hands, hard, like cold stones. The nights he was too much in his cups, or in polite company, it was with words. I'd been called stupid and worthless for so long I'd almost come to believe it.

No wonder I'd turned out the way I had. Put someone in charge of me, and I'll buck like a wild horse. Give me a gun and I'll hurt whoever you point me at. Hand me a bottle, and

I'll try to drown in it. Anything to be away from those memories, the things you can't talk about. Men'll just turn it into a pissing match, and women don't want to hear about a man's hurt when they've enough of their own. Pain's a poison well, not to be shared unless you expect to kill another's spirit.

But my boys, they didn't deserve that, and I'd made a vow they would never know it. If violence needed to be done, gods willing, I'd be doing it instead of them. And they would never see the hard side of my hands. A man ain't a man if he can't best someone the size of a sapling without words.

A light rain began to fall, and Anne pulled close. She held one arm across her ribs, nursing a split lip and a black eye. I pulled the whiskey out, my body starting to holler again. I took a swig and handed it over. She gave me a look of thanks and took a long swallow as well.

"How we gonna collect on that bounty?" She asked once the liquor settled in.

I looked up. The clouds were still thin and gray, nothing like the black thunderheads that threatened the greater prairie when a storm whipped up. Tilted my head down again.

"How d'ya mean?"

"We can't get to the girls. What kinda proof we got to have, anyway?"

I looked over. "You didn't ask?"

She blushed. "Was a bit busy."

"Mmhm. I reckon we take these boys' ears, then. As far as turning it in, Cora'll be tending Kent. She'll take it."

"What about the law?"

I spat. "Fuck the law."

The rain started to come a little harder, tamping down the trail dust. A stand of cottonwoods huddled nearby, and we rode under it, dismounting. This far from town, the Creek had turned to a river, and flowed in a gentle rush toward the east. I tied the horses off and fed them while Anne laid out the bedrolls. I brushed Drafter and then her horse, murmuring soothing words while thunder rumbled overhead. When I finished, I joined her.

She handed me a strip of jerky and a crust of bread with a tin cup of water. We ate in silence. When we'd finished, I laid back on my bedroll and watched the clouds through the canopy. The gentle pitter-pat of rain off leaves was soothing, and I closed my eyes.

"You really mean to take their ears?" Anne asked quietly.

I sighed. My damn mouth. Did I? Maybe. It was certainly something the old Wil would have done. There were things I didn't tell Ginny, no matter her policy on keeping secrets. There are things I don't think you can be forgiven for. I sometimes wondered why I didn't leave the place where I'd seen and caused so much death. Where we'd broken the land, and even the earth seemed to hate us.

I should've just taken Ginny and the boys and moved south. Maybe it was stubborn determination. My father was hell-bent on convincing me I was a failure. I wanted—needed—to prove him wrong. I carried that over to my fight against the Church. Doing my best to prove I was in the right, and even if I wasn't, that I wasn't failing at being wrong. Even when they threw me in that hole, I was determined to thrive, even if the way I did it was broken.

A little sliver of doubt crept in, like ice in my heart, and I wondered if Ginny had ever been disappointed in me. Or if she hid it, buried it deep. She'd always supported me, no matter how wrong-headed my decisions. I wondered then what it was she had really wanted. She'd always claimed it was to be with me, no matter where or circumstances, but surely, she was more than the fever dream of a wicked man? And I hadn't seen it.

When the rain broke through the leaves and dripped onto my face, I let it hide the tears sneaking from under my lids.

"Wil?" Anne asked. "You still awake?"

I cleared my throat. "Yeah."

"You really mean to take their ears?" She asked again.

She sounded scared. I thought about how young she was. Wondered what set her down this path. Remembered my own. Remembered my boys.

"We'll take something. Maybe they got identification of some sort."

I heard her let out a slow sigh. Didn't want to let me know she was worried. I didn't blame her. Some steps you take on a path are ones you can't take back. They change who you are at your core.

"Wil?" She said again into the silence.

I sighed. "Yeah?"

"Where'd you get those tattoos?"

"Go to sleep, Anne."

"All right, you old mule. 'Night."

"'Night."

I turned my head and let the sound of rain lull me to sleep.

Five

"Where'd you get those tattoos?" Anne asked again once we were back on the trail.

I sighed. "Not gonna let this go, are you?"

"Like a dog with a bone."

I opened my mouth for a reply.

"Not your shriveled bone."

Closed it. She was getting some of her old spunk back. That was good. A person with no fire got no reason to fight. I let her have her dig. I was feeling pretty good, anyway. My ribs had let up a little. Tender to the touch, but I'd managed not to knock them around too much. Maybe it was the whiskey, but I wasn't arguing. I decided to give a little.

"I'm a Null," I said.

"Thought they was all dead."

"Church tried. Callers don't like us."

We rode a bit further, passing through an arroyo whose floor was already a fast-running stream. The rain hadn't let up yet, and the desert was beginning to bloom: green shoots the color of emeralds, pink flowers, lizards the size of my pinkie darting about.

"What's a Null, anyway?" Anne asked.

"We're dead spaces in the Empyrean. We can make things..." I waved a hand. It was harder to explain than do. "We can stop magic. Callers tap the Empyrean, we reach through it because it avoids us. Sometimes we can make a tunnel and take the center out of things."

"Yeah? Like kill them?"

I shrugged. "Sure."

"Why didn't you do it back in the Creek when they was beating the shit outta us, then?"

"I haven't used it much in years. And every time you open a gate, something pushes back. It wants out. Small things—rocks, cans, some animals—don't have much of a center, so you don't need a big gate to reach through. Men are big. Horses, too. The bigger the tunnel, the more likely whatever's on the other side is gonna get free. To take out those men, I would've likely let something loose that would've killed the whole town."

"You ever open a big gate?"

"Yeah, once."

"What happened?"

"Everybody died."

"Don't sound like somethin' somebody'd want truck with, then."

"Yeah. Church feels the same way."

The trail moved uphill, and we rode out onto a flat plain of hardpan. Herds moved in the distance, great lizards the ranchers raised for food. The buttes gave way to mesas painted in a variety of reds, oranges, and yellows. Succulents, sagebrush, and cottonwood thrived. A small ranch sat nearby. Farmhouse, corrals, and toolsheds all surrounded by a fence. The rain slackened, and I cursed.

"What?" Anne asked.

"Was hoping for a good rain to hide us. On a good day, you can see to the sea from here. Didn't want nobody to see us coming."

As if I'd called him into being, a rider appeared from the north, moving at a good clip. I loosened my pistol in its holster, and saw Anne do the same from the corner of my eye. The rider veered our way until he was close enough to make out details. Longcoat, three-piece suit. White hair flying from beneath his hat as he kicked the horse to a gallop. He drew closer, and I let my palm rest on the butt of my pistol. Ben grinned and tipped his cap up a little, then spurred the horse away, toward a piece of hardpan where mirage lines rose in waves.

"Ah, shit," I said.

"What?" Anne asked.

"He's headed for a deadland."

"Why?"

"Might be stupid. Might be he's planning on drawing it out toward the ranch. Which would be stupid as well."

Anne grunted. "Got balls on him."

I nodded. "Yeah, that's about it, I reckon."

Deadlands were where magic and null had clashed, and the souls of the men killed remained trapped between here and the Empyrean. Even as we watched, they rose, screaming, clutching remembered wounds. They grasped at Ben's horse, but he was moving too fast, and instead, they gave chase. It was said the dead are ravenous, and in this case, I believed it.

"Should we help?" Anne asked.

"No," I said. "C'mon."

I spurred Drafter in the other direction, coming at the Henrick ranch from the south. I hoped they'd be too busy with Ben and the trouble he'd stirred up to notice us.

We hadn't quite circled around to the back of the ranch, and I saw Ben's horse stumble, its foreleg caught in a prairie dog hole. The horse screamed as the leg snapped, sending Ben flying. The ghosts caught up, tearing the poor animal to shreds as it bleated in terror. Men scrambled from the ranch, grabbing their would-be hunter from the desert floor and dragging him inside the fence line.

"Fuck," I cursed. I hoped they'd be occupied enough to miss us. We made the fence and tied our horses off, then slipped under the rails. I had my pistol out, and Anne hers as we crept along the backside of the sheds. Voices slowed, then halted us. I peered around the side of an outbuilding, Anne jostling me for room.

Three men stood in a semicircle, their backs to us. Their leader was roughly the size of an outhouse. Two more had hold of Ben's arms, stretching him out. He'd lost his hat in the tumble, and his hair hung over his face in stringy locks. The big man held a hatchet in one hand.

"How many of you?" He asked Ben.

Ben looked up blearily. Someone had stripped him of his guns. He was going to die here if we didn't do something.

"Just me," he coughed.

"And you came for all of us? Shit son, I don't know if that's brave or stupid. Especially over some whores."

"Ain't whores," Ben mumbled.

The leader tipped his chin up. "What?" he asked.

"You gotta do something," Anne whispered in my ear. I shushed her with a wave of my hand.

"Ain't whores. They're ladies," Ben said, a little louder.

The big man spat into the dirt. "Stupid, losing your arm over a whore," he said.

He raised the hatchet. I saw my chance. A bullet in the back of the head would do for him quick. I thought about my boys and how I'd have to split that money four ways if Ben lived. And I made my choice.

The hatchet came down, severing Ben's left arm. The man howled as blood poured from the wound in a torrent. Spittle clung to his lips like a spiderweb as he screamed. He tipped over and lay in the dirt, coughing and weeping, clutching the stump like he could put his life back in. His fingers went slick, and they slipped from the exposed meat. The dust around him went a deep muddy red.

I put that bullet in the back of the big man's head, then. My next two shots went wide. Anne stepped around the corner and took two more of the men in the guts. They went down with grunts like they'd been punched in the stomach.

The other two scattered, and I wasted another two bullets just trying to hit one.

"Where?" Anne screamed.

I pointed to the outhouse. They'd holed up behind it and were taking potshots at us. I ducked back behind the toolshed.

"Keep 'em there," I said.

Anne nodded. She looked like someone had crept up and shit her britches when she wasn't looking. Still, she was holding up for now. I went to the far end of the shed and started to flank the boys. One popped out and tried to take a shot, but Anne hammered him back with a quick round into the outhouse door.

I'd reached another shed just to the side of the outhouse. All it would take was me rounding the corner. I took a breath. I couldn't shoot for shit these days—the girl hadn't been wrong about that—but at this range, I likely couldn't miss. I just needed to distract them.

"Why don't you boys give up now?" I called.

"Ain't givin' up for no whore's lapdog," one called back.

"You'd rather die than sit in jail for a bit?"

No answer. They were either thinking about it, or creeping up on me.

I spun around the corner. One of the boys, a bit on the heavy side, was still peering in Anne's direction. I put a bullet in the back of his neck. When his partner turned, I put one through his sternum. They dropped into the dust, sending little clouds up. The ranch was quiet again. I stepped from hiding and around Ben's body. Looked down at him a moment. He stared back from clouded eyes gone still. Poor stupid bastard.

I knelt beside the bodies and rummaged through their trousers. Anne did the same. Not a thing on them. I grabbed the older boy's knife and got to cutting. Ears come away easy. Anne watched, green as grass. When I finished, I tucked the ears away into a bag, and we made our way back to the horses.

"Shouldn't we bury them?" Anne asked. Her voice shook.

"Coyotes need to eat, too," I said.

I spurred Drafter, and we rode back toward the Creek.

We stopped again in the copse of cottonwoods beside the trail. The day had turned muggy, threatening rain again, and my ribs ached with the adrenaline wearing off. I climbed off Drafter and let Anne take care of the horses while I built a small fire. I dug some food out for us and the whiskey and set to drinking.

By the time she came out of the shadows where we'd tethered our mounts, her eyes were red. I handed her the dried meat and bread, but she just gave them a hollow look.

"Need to eat," I said. "Still a ride back."

"I ain't never killed no one," she said. "Does it get easier?"

I thought about that. I'd killed my share of men over the years, both in the war, and for the merc companies. The things I'd done in prison—they might have been counted as mercies, but that was splitting hairs. Was I different for it? Maybe. Could I have been a better man without it? Probably.

I shook my head. "Not easier, just different. You just learn not to dwell on it. Instinct takes over. You learn there are no easy choices but the one you're handed when someone's going to kill you."

"But they had their backs turned."

"Yeah, maybe. You think they wouldn't have done the same to you?" I looked at her. "Maybe after making some sport of you, first. You knew what them men had done."

She sniffled. "You let Ben die."

"Yeah, I did."

"Why?"

"Sometimes you have to make hard choices."

Silence fell between us. The stars crept out from behind the veil of night, and I laid back in my bedroll. Her voice came one more time before sleep took over, small and far away.

"Don't think I want any of this. Think I'll take my money and go home."

"First good choice you've made," I said.

She didn't reply.

Six

Morning found me sitting on a log, inspecting the new pistol. I had a few shells left—enough for a couple reloads. I wondered idly if the general store in the Creek sold these now. Easy to load, easy to shoot. More efficient killing. Hard to argue with.

Anne crawled from her bedroll bleary-eyed and set to working on the jerky from the night before. I cleaned the barrel and the chambers best I could and gave the pistol a good oil before I loaded it back up. The Hennick boy's knife I'd slipped into my belt, at the small of my back.

I looked at her, thought about what she must be feeling.

"Why'd you want this money?" I asked.

She laughed, a bitter sound. "Wanted to be famous. Wanted to get me one of those fancy rifles and tour competitions. Make a name for myself."

"Still want that?"

She chewed, eyes far off. Finally, she shook her head.

"Nah," she said, voice just above a whisper. "Just want to go home. See my ma and pa. Sorry, Wil."

I dug out the whiskey and handed her the bottle. She looked at it, took a swallow.

"Does it get easier?" She asked, echoing herself from the night before.

"In time," I said.

I didn't know if that's what she needed to hear, but if it kept her from eating a bullet, it was what I'd tell her. Killing never got easier. It just got different. The guilt came less often. The revulsion. That feeling like you're dirty so deep you could peel off the top layers and still be filthy fades into the background.

"You got a wife?" Anne asked, changing the subject.

I thought about what Ginny might have thought of the things I'd done on this ride. Pushed it away. She was cold in the ground, and I had boys to care for.

"Gone," I said. "Croup got her."

"Kids?"

"Two. Boys."

"Yeah? You do this for them, then?"

"Yeah."

Did I? The Wil who left those men to rot on the ground wasn't the Wil his family would recognize. I might have needed the money for my family, but what I did back there was to prove a point. To myself and Dag. I refused to let the Church tell me what's right, even all these years later, and especially from the lips of a jumped-up lawman. I'd nearly died for that cause, and I still believed in it. I finished loading the pistol and snapped the cylinder shut, then slipped the gun in its holster.

Anne watched me for a moment, then held out her own pistol. I looked at it, then her.

"What?"

"Take it," she said, urging it toward me like it was a snake that might bite her.

I shook my head. "Keep it. If you can't shoot no more, sell it. It'll bring you some cash."

She nodded and slipped it back into its holster.

"Time to go," I said.

I packed up our gear while she finished eating. We saddled up and rode out, horse's hooves sinking a little in the soft earth. The desert had come into full bloom, and thick clusters of clover shone emerald. Pink and purple and orange flowers blossomed everywhere, and life, small and large, darted across the earth. The air grew heavier as we moved east, and great clouds gathered like anvils over the plain.

The outskirts of the Creek came into sight as the sun sank, thunder chasing the last of the light away. As we neared, new construction drew our eye. A gibbet had been erected at the crossroads, a body swinging in the wind. Loops of intestine hung between its legs like festival bunting.

I tugged on Drafter's reins as we drew close, bringing the old horse to a halt. Kent swung from the noose. Someone had hung a sign around his neck reading: LAWBREAKER. The old rage spread across my heart, brittle and cold like winter ice. I'd known Kent a long time. Longer even than Ginny. To see him, snuffed so carelessly... I turned to Anne, and she recoiled from my gaze.

"Get the whore. Don't let them see you. I want our money. I want Kent's share, too."

"What're you gonna do?" She asked.

"Best you not know. I've got business in town."

Anne nodded and rode for the Creek like all the devils of hell were on her ass. Maybe they were. I waited until she dwindled into the night, and then made for the old bunkhouse on the outskirts. Rain, in fat cold drops, drummed the ground and lightning split the sky, thunder roaring after.

I hitched Drafter around back and went inside. The bunkhouse showed no signs of a scuffle. They'd likely taken Kent when he was still out, strung him up then. I thought of all the things we'd done together. Wanted to spend some time eulogizing him properly. Instead of words, I could only grasp my own hate for the Church and the man who'd killed him.

Kent's long gun leaned against one of the clapboards. I picked it up, hefted it. Still loaded. After a moment of thought, I went to the old boarded-up window, and pried one of the pine slats away, then settled in, rifle resting on the sill. Something told me I wouldn't have to go to them.

The storm raged, lightning and thunder and wind, rain smashing into roof and siding. I peered out into the night. Lightning slashed the dark, and memory did the same.

All of us huddled in the house, a plains rager howling around the eaves. Ginny rocked in her chair, trying to show the boys it didn't scare her. Her hands worked her needlepoint, in the canvas, out. In the canvas, out. Still, I caught the slight quaver, the hitch when thunder shook the windows in their panes. She looked up and caught me watching. Gave a sly smile.

"You ain't got nothin' better to do, big man?"

I grinned back, hugged the boys closer. I looked down at them.

"You boys scared?"

"No sir," they piped up.

"Why's that? Is it because you're clever or brave?" I asked.

"Brave, sir," Carter said.

"Ain't nothin' but giants clapping, papa," Fallon said.

"Yeah? Well, I think your ma could use a little bravery."

"Wil Cutter, don't you start no nonsense," she warned.

"I think she could use some real strong boys to keep her tight in that chair. What d'you think?"

The boys giggled, and despite Ginny's protests, piled onto her rocker, one on her knees, the other at her arm, hugging her tight. She looked out from the pile-on with mock outrage.

"Wil, if you don't call your hounds off—"

I got up and stalked over, my grin wider than ever.

"What're you up to—" The question rose to a hysterical shriek as I set to tickling her. She dissolved into laughter, calling my name between breaths.

"Wil! Wil! WIL CUTTER!"

The memory shattered and the voice came again.

I looked out the window. Dag and his boys—four of 'em—stood out in the storm, iron on their hips. Anne stood just behind them with an ashamed look, like a child caught in a lie. I knew then she'd turned coat. I sighted down the barrel of the long gun.

"I'm sorry, Wil!" Anne called. "I didn't want to kill them boys. I just needed the money!"

I grunted and shot her in the gut. She went down with a wail of despair and pain. Never could abide traitors. I moved the sights over to Dag, who had already raised his arm, tattoos shining wet in the storm's light. I didn't realize what he was doing until a blue bolt struck from above, hitting the rifle and blowing it out of my hands.

It misfired, ricochets sending splinters flying about the interior of the room. It blasted me back as well, sending me skidding across the floor until my spine fetched up against the far wall. My teeth hurt, the stink of burnt hair filling my nostrils. My ribs screamed, and I puked up my meager breakfast.

"Fuck!" I roared.

Two of Dag's deputies kicked in the door and came for me, pistols out. I pulled mine free with tingling fingers. The first shot took the lead man in the eye and his head rocked back, spraying his partner with brains.

As his body dropped, I shot the second in the knee. He went down but managed to fire his own weapon. The bullet nicked my ear, sending blood cascading down into my shirt.

I returned the favor and blew his skull wide like a cactus blossom.

Dag's magic must've woken something in me. I felt him charge the next blast and reached out with my Null, causing the lightning to sizzle before it started. He cursed, and two more of his boys showed up. One in the window, firing like he was blind and pissed.

The shots tore chunks out of the room. I dove up under him and pulled the knife from my belt, slamming it through his chin and into his brain. He made a *gluk gluk gluk* sound and keeled over.

The last had crept in over his dead companions and caught me in the hip—another grazing shot, but deep enough to send a line of agonizing fire through my leg. I rolled onto my back and shot him twice in the chest. Blood poured from his mouth, and he coughed once, lung full of his own fluids. He died choking.

Quiet for a moment. I peeked up over the sill. Dag's bullet ripped a splinter of wood away and shattered a piece of broken glass still clinging to it.

"I told you we don't cotton to lawbreakers here," Dag called. "You come out now, you might get a fair trial."

I fumbled bullets into the pistol. My last rounds. I didn't think I'd need them, though. I'd seen something in the mud, where the rain was washing away the top layers like a river erodes a bank.

Dag fired another shot into the bunkhouse. It hit with a dull thud.

"You know, you took out four good men. We could use men like you. You throw your gun out, and we'll talk about it."

Predictable as hell. I tossed the gun through the doorway. He fired four more shots, shattering the doorframe. Six shots. He'd have to reload. I had to move. I rounded the corner, hands out. We stood in the mud. Dag's foot slipped, and he righted himself without looking down. I saw the bones there, the skull he'd slid on.

"You want justice, right?" I asked.

"Yeah, justice," Dag agreed.

He reloaded his pistol bullet by bullet. Sign of a pro. Slow is fast and fast is smooth. Cold rain, too easy to slip, lose a bullet in the mud. I lowered my arms, sleeves falling over my tattoos. I ignited them with a thought. Felt the Empyrean on the other side. Eager, hungry. I started opening the gates. Not too much. If he twigged to it, I'd be dead in a heartbeat.

"Was what you did to Kent justice?"

"Was what you did to that girl?"

"Ain't no honor for traitors."

"She just wanted to go home, Wil."

He snapped the cylinder shut.

"Yeah, so did Kent," I said. "So do I."

I opened the gates. Bigger than I had in years. And the dead came. They screamed through from the Empyrean, taking hold of the bones, dragging themselves free. Dag lowered the pistol to shoot me, then realized what I'd done. His expression changed to pure horror. His professional façade slipped, and he started firing into the dead. Bones shattered; skeletons collapsed. I opened the gates wider, and something in the desert answered. Something big and nasty.

"You're gonna kill us all!" Dag shouted.

"That's the idea," I said.

He lifted the pistol again to shoot me down, and I turned away. I half-expected a bullet in the back. What I got was Dag, screaming wetly as the dead pulled him apart. I went around back of the bunkhouse, picking up Kent's rifle along the way. I saddled up Drafter. Gave it some thought and led the horse around front. By then, the night had gone quiet. What was left of Dag was a stain in the mud. I walked over to Anne, knelt beside her. She was still alive. I rooted through her trousers until I found the bounty. Can't trust anyone these days.

She coughed and reached for me, and I kicked her hand away. I looked up. Something vast and bone-white lurched for the town, its shadow falling over the outbuildings. A horror from an earlier time. I looked down at her, at the tears pouring from her eyes.

"It's only gonna hurt for a little while," I said.

I saddled up and rode away, leaving the Creek to its fate.

Seven

After the abomination had passed, and the town was a smoldering ruin, I rode to the crossroads and cut Kent down. It was the least I could do. I wrapped him in his coat and took him to Tika.

The prairie was quiet, a sort of hush as it waited for the first snows to fall. I thought again of the things we'd been through.

We were six weeks out of Yuma when the train came through. Full of prisoners, it was headed east, to the capital. Gods only knew what the Church had planned for them. Me, Kent, and six other men had laid dynamite over the tracks. When they blew, it send a shudder through the earth, kicking up dirt and smoke and twisted metal. Then we hunkered down to wait.

The train came down the tracks like a great iron horse, smoke pouring from its stack like it was possessed of a demon. The engineer must've seen the wreckage before he could derail, and hit the brakes, steel on steel squealing like the Devil's fiddle. The train juddered to a halt, and the engineer got off to inspect the damage ahead. One of the boys caught him high in the head with a bullet, his skull exploding into a pink mist.

Three others disembarked the train, Callers all. I shut them down with the Null and Kent picked them off one by one. The rest of the guards were just Church troopers, and though they were wearing that ceramic armor they favored, they must've been green. Probably thought no one would hit a train full of undesirables.

By the time we were done, we'd liberated some forty men, women, and children. One of the few times in the war I'd been proud of what I'd done.

The memory faded, and I found myself beside another copse of trees. I stopped there for the night, laying Kent out beside the fire. Not sure why I did it, other than thinking maybe he was cold.

I lay in my bedroll, watching the clouds and stars pass overhead. Somewhere, a coyote called out. I half expected Kent to say something. When he didn't, my heart sank, and I looked over. He was still in his shroud. Always would be. I closed my eyes and let the dark wash over me.

The next morning, I saddled up and took him the rest of the way home. Snow had begun to spit from the sky in fat flakes, and the few birds wheeling above spent little time in the air before seeking shelter from the gusting wind.

I reached his homestead by midday, Tika coming out to greet me. She took one look at my single horse, and the bundle over my saddle and let out a cry of anguish. She ran to me, beating my chest with her fists. I let her. This was my fault.

When she finished, I helped her dig the grave beside the creek. The soil here was softer, more amenable to planting. Somewhere in the fields, a head of cattle lowed. When we were done, I looked at the bed of soil we'd made, thinking of another back home. I'd already dug too many graves and it hadn't even been a month. I hoped to dig no more.

I looked over at Tika, still standing beside Kent's cairn. She looked up at me with red-rimmed eyes. I walked over and handed her Kent's share of the bounty, and a little more for watching the boys.

"Go," was all she said.

I nodded, pulled my hat on, and saddled up. I rode away from the ranch, feeling less welcome in this world than since the war.

The cold had crept in fully, and snow rode the wind like ash. My memory flashed again, to entering a town where the people greeted us as heroes. I wondered if in another life, I might have been a good man. I wondered if I could give that to my boys. The wind picked up, and I wrapped the coat around myself, and spurred Drafter down the trail.

Smoke. It rose in a thick plume, pulled to the south by a hungry wind. Fat flakes of snow rode winter breath and I spurred Drafter toward the source. Smoke meant fire, and fire meant disaster, especially this late in the season. I cursed the boys, hoping they hadn't burned the whole stead down.

Drafter's hooves pounded the snow flat as we galloped, and I thought about the ride Kent and I had in Dumai, the Rangers coming up against a Church detachment. We'd seen the smoke from six miles off, it coming off adobe homes like a plague. By the time our patrol had got there, wasn't much left but bodies and ash. It lay inches thick, in some cases covering our horses' fetlocks.

They'd burned the fields and homes, and where the people from Dumai had tried to run or stand their ground, they cut them down and burned them, too. What had maybe once been women huddled in doorways and behind charred doors, the flesh black and crispy, red where it had split from the heat. The babies were bloated like they'd spent days in the sun, the men little more than featureless husks where heat had melted flesh and fat to tallow.

The plume grew in size, from a whirlwind to a tornado, and I pulled up short, Drafter skidding in the new snow. The stead was a charred skeleton, the roof caved in like sagging ribs. The crops had blackened and withered in the heat. I flew from the saddle and ran for the door hanging like a broken tooth.

Two shapes, still small, dusted in snow, black peering through the white, stopped me short. I couldn't look. Didn't. I knew what that black was, had seen flesh charred before, seen the white of bone where the fat had run off, red cracks where the skin had split from the heat. I puked into the drifts the wind had stirred up, staggered, found my knees. Where my heart should have been, where it had been ice, was now just a hollow, as if someone had scooped that organ out and replaced it with nothing. I was used to the cut-glass ache of pain, the jagged cold of hate, but this—

The man sitting on the still-smoldering steps walked over and crouched, hands dangling between his knees. Dimly, I became aware of others—ten, maybe fifteen—carrying rifles and pistols, and the blue and white of the Church. The man in front of me—I tried to focus, but the snow was in my face, melting on my lashes and cheeks.

"Welcome home, Wil," he said.

And then someone pistol-whipped me, and the world went black.

Eight

When I woke, two things came to me.

Cold. Like I'd not felt in a long while, the kind that creeps into fingers and toes and joints and makes you ache like someone set you aflame—I vomited down the side of the horse I was tied to, bile splattering the ground in thick yellow gobbets, the wind sweeping it under as it pushed the snow.

Pain. My ribs screamed in agony with every jostle and bounce, and my skull throbbed like someone had been at it with a hammer. And then, deeper, in my chest, agony like I'd never known. I thought I was dying, and tears worked from my eyes, froze to my cheeks. I hadn't even got to dig the graves. All that violence, for what?

Rage followed, a red wave, and I reached for the Empyrean. I meant to open a hole big enough to swallow me, to swallow the world. I concentrated, opened my will, and... nothing. The man riding beside me tutted, and I saw the tattoos around his wrists, the same as mine. I snarled in animal instinct.

"Turncoat," I spat.

"War's over, Wil," he said.

Something in the back of my head echoed in remembrance, and I craned my neck to see who was speaking. He was a tall man, brown skin, beard showing white on a sharp jawline.

"Fletcher," I said. "They turned you after all. How's it feel to be a lapdog?"

"Better than it feels to be a dead man walking," he said.

We rode in silence for a time. I craned my neck now and again to see where we were headed, or at least where we were. The group made good time and the plains gave way to wooded foothills. Mountains loomed to the north, tall, jagged peaks where the snow never left and pine clung to the sides like ticks on a dog. We rode a quiet forest trail, pine, maple, oak, and birch huddled together as if they felt the cold.

"What'd they offer you?" I asked. "You get a fresh pair of boots to lick every morning?"

He grinned, as if it was all a joke. My misery, what he'd done to my children, where we were going. I knew already. I'd ridden this path once before, just after the war.

"A warm home, amnesty, and a steady paycheck. I got three meals and I don't want. Can you say the same?" He looked me in the eye then and scoffed. "Don't suppose you can." Turned back to the trail.

"You know what the Church teaches about men like you, Wil?" He asked.

"You know what the Church teaches about men like us, Fletcher? Damned is damned. You just chose the coward's path."

"Maybe. But a live coward is better than brave and dead.

You know the difference between bravery and stupidity, Wil?"

"I have the feeling you're gonna tell me, child-killer."

He snapped his mouth shut, brow beetling.

"You killed them kids, Wil. The things you did, the Church passed sentence."

"And you put them to the flame."

"I was just following orders."

"That's what they said in Dumai. You remember Dumai, don't you, Fletch?"

He clenched his jaw until I saw the striations in the muscle. After a long moment, he spoke again.

"Save your energy. You're gonna need it in the Pit."

We cleared the trees and he spurred his horse to the front of the line. I listened to the hoofbeats recede, and when they were gone, lifted my head again. We'd come upon a wide rocky clearing, trees on all sides. Guard shacks stood at each cardinal direction, a steel fence strung between them in a circle wide enough to swallow a battalion. Just inside, a stockhouse and a barracks. In the center, a hole. Black and deep and spiraling, each level cold and hard and deadly.

Fletcher's men rode through the guard post and dismounted. They untied me from the horse and marched me to a rickety wooden platform hanging over the empty space like a threat. A crane supported it, alongside which was a massive spool of rope piled beside the gantry. They shoved me atop the platform and unspooled the rope. I plummeted, holding onto the edges as it fell into the bowels of the earth. No ceremony, no trial, no mercy.

Eventually, the descent slowed, and I knew I was into the guts of the pit. But they meant to drop me into the lowest levels. The places where the sun don't ever reach. It was an execution. If the Church believed that those who were born unable to touch the Empyrean were damned from birth, this was as close to Hell as they could get you without outright sending you there themselves.

I clung to the edges of the platform, not caring if the earth opened up wholly and swallowed me. I had nothing left to give, nothing left to lose. A man can be broken any number of ways, but the easiest is to let him rise just a little above his birth, then tear it away. A part of me knew what Fletcher'd told me was true. That I'd killed my boys as sure as if I'd held the blade myself. Killing Dag had pretty much signed that writ.

Thing is, when you find yourself with family, consequences fall to the side at times. You'd do anything to keep them safe, fed, and warm. To give them the things you never had. Maybe that's not true of everyone, but it was for me. I'd never been a good man, so when Ginny'd come along, I'd tried all that much harder to be. Lesser concerns didn't trouble me on that path. Things like others standing in my way. Though, that had never been the heaviest weight on my shoulders.

The platform came to a halt, thumping into the stony earth. I raised my head enough to see darkness on each side, the light above a hazy ball. A creaking sound filled the air, and one side of the platform loosed, dumping me on the ground. The wood dangled on its side as it was raised, and soon passed out of sight.

I sat and dug my fingers in to the dirt. Felt the cool loose grains rasp against my palms, felt the smooth hardness of rock. I remembered Ginny. On her knees in the yard. I'd dug and tilled and broke sod until we had a suitable patch for growing, and then brought her seeds from the Creek. She pulled me from my spot on the porch.

"C'mon old man," she said, a twinkle in her eye.

"What is it now?" I was tired and out of sorts.

"Time you learned something."

"I dug you rows already, woman."

"Somethin' that ain't shootin' or plowin'."

"Never heard you complain," I muttered as I found my feet.

"I heard that. Keep sassin' me and you'll be plowing by hand."

"Yes'm," I said, properly chastised, and followed her to where I'd turned sod to loam, furrows breaking the earth.

She knelt and reached into one of those little paper pouches, pressed the seed into the soil with her finger, then scooped more dirt over it. When she was done, she did it again, and again. When she was halfway up the row, she stopped and looked at me from under her big floppy hat.

"I swear to gods, Cutter, if you don't get down here, you'll be eating potatoes until next spring."

"Sorry, I was admirin'," I said.

"Flattery will get you the rest of the row."

She stood and handed me the packet of seeds. I sighed and knelt, and we planted a whole row together, her guiding my hand to the right depth, and showing me just how to build the earth so it wasn't too tight but still kept the seed safe. When we finished, she fell back and mopped her forehead, fanning herself with her hat.

"Not bad," she said.

"Yeah? Would you say I'm pretty good at planting seed?"

She smiled and leaned in, took my hand and put it on her belly. "Not bad at all," she whispered in my ear.

Joy filled me. Then despair as the memory faded and I remembered the man I'd been. The man I'd become again. I clutched the soil of the prison floor and fell back, watching the light above dim by degrees.

Man in a hole has a lot of time to think. A lot of time to watch the disc of light at the top of the world slide away, giving way to star-decked night. I thought about whether I wanted to live. This deep in the Pit, I didn't even know if it was a possibility. No guards walked these levels, no food made it down. If you survived, and judging by the distinct lack of life this deep you likely wouldn't; would you want to? Eking out a living on what? Roots and grubs? Would I want to go on that way? Bereft of home and family, broken. I felt as dead inside as those I'd left behind.

Black thoughts led to black memory. I thought about the war. The Church wanted people like me dead. They'd subverted the Council, slithered their way into the halls of power, like weeds in the rows. And once they'd put their roots deep, they strangled the old guard and acted. We'd banded together. The Nulls and their families, sympathizers, under Farson's banner. We'd fought.

But the Church—they had the technology. Airships powered by the Empyrean, Callers in armor that stopped nearly everything thrown at them. Weapons capable of channeling arcane energy, scorching entire cities.

It was winter near the end. They'd cornered us in the woods, not far from the Pit itself. Trapped between plains blizzards and impassable mountains, we hunkered down in the trees and prayed for a miracle. None came. They had us surrounded. They'd sent men in, but we knew the land, knew the way it lay and the hollows and dry creeks. We knew how to kill when they came. But we didn't know how to escape. So, they waited us out.

We took to eating our dead before the snows ended. We took to a great many things a man should never have to endure. And when we knew we could wait no more, we opened a gate. Three of us. The biggest damn gate the world had ever known. And it broke… everything.

When it passed, the remnants of our forces came together, blood and bone and steel and raw hate. We killed and killed until we couldn't kill no more, and then they took the survivors, and they dropped us here, in the Pit.

One of those three died on the way. I killed another—the man who'd given Kent his scars. The violence didn't concern them as long as we were contained. We were damned, but we were damned at their leisure.

Curiosity got the better of me, and I tried to open a gate. I felt a trickle of power, the Empyrean flowing away from me in feeble waves. Whatever they did in this place kept Nulls' power at a nadir.

Movement caught the corner of my eye and I turned my head, dirt rasping against my skull. Something pale and faintly translucent shuffled from the dark. I walked with a hunch and wielded what could only be a femur. Great black eyes protruded from above a noseless face. Its mouth was split in a razor grin.

I cursed softly and tried to work myself to a defensible position. There are degrees to wanting to die, and I didn't want it to be to these things. I'd seen them once before, in Dumai, after the Church had moved on. They were scavengers, carrion beasts who ate human flesh. Living or dead, they weren't picky. Another came from my right, and I managed to find my feet, head and ribs throbbing. Rest had done me some good, but it would be a while before I was whole again.

I moved, hoping to at least get my back against a wall. I stumbled as I went, my bootheel catching on something that clattered in the dark, and I stooped, eyes still on the stalkers. My hand found the jagged edge of a bone, and I grasped it like a long knife.

The stalkers kept coming, and I found the wall. I'd gotten lucky. Normally they moved in packs. No one knew quite where they came from, but suspicion was that they were borne from the tear in the Empyrean we'd made. They seemed to be able to walk straight from the shadows into just about anywhere where there'd been a death. And this place had seen plenty.

A shout from above, echoed by more, answered that question. There was a commotion on the tiers, and a pale body suddenly fell, still silent. I saw my chance and darted left.

The creature on my right read it as panic and charged forward. It was flattened by its falling companion, the two bodies colliding and exploding like wet sacks of meat. Their slime spattered me, and I spat a chunk of the foul flesh out.

The creature before me twitched its gaze to the side and I lunged, broken bone extended, and impaled it in the stomach. It dropped its own weapon and looked down as if confused. Its hands wrapped around the shaft, and I gave the knob of bone a solid kick with my heel, driving it out the thing's back. It collapsed, eyes going blank.

I stood, shaking with adrenaline, then sat heavy in the dirt. It seemed I did want to live.

Little by little I became aware of the noise on the tiers above. They'd been attacked as well. I wondered what it would take to set this whole place off.

When I felt a little more whole, I grabbed a broken bone, and with the methodical work of a man with nothing but time on his hands, pulled the stalkers into a pile and started to carve handholds in the earthen wall.

Winter was closing in. I knew it in the way the days were shorter, the tiny patch of blue above paler. It was cold, even this far down, insulated from the worst of it. But I knew all it would take was one good snow, one good sleet, and the whole of my dig would turn to mud and I'd be trapped until it hardened up.

I dug for a week; the days filled with gnawing hunger. I popped fat grubs and slurped down their insides, took small sips of my own piss, and when desperate enough, of the stalkers' blood. It did little to slake the thirst and hunger, but it kept me going.

Each night, the stalkers visited. I killed them and heaped their bodies in a stinking pile in the center of the floor. When it got too cold to dig, and my hands cracked and bled and new blisters formed, I set to work on the bodies before they were useless.

I was lucky. I'd never been this close to a stalker before, and it was a shock to learn they didn't decompose like men. I cut the flesh of their bellies away with the sharp edge of a bone, then the muscle. They bled only a little, and what there was was milky and pale. I cut their tendons and shattered more bone until I found was able to make a crude needle. I looked at it a long moment, thinking of Ginny and her needlepoint, and tried to recall the motions she made as she stitched.

My first few tries failed. I tore the flesh. The tendon strings were too thick, or too thin. Same with the skin. Lucky for me, there were plenty of the dead. On the fourth day, I got it right, but could only throw a few stitches before hunger nearly bowled me over.

I did what I had to. Stalker meat is stringy. Their blood salty and bitter. But it kept me alive. I ate and I puked, and I ate again, and then I rested. When I felt better, I finished the crude mittens, slipping them onto my hands. They felt rough and strange, but they'd work. The skin was strong and supple and gripped well. I tried not to think too hard about it.

My wounds were finally starting to heal, the constant exercise strengthening muscle long gone fallow. By the fifth week, I had two good bones for digging, and about twenty feet of handholds. Of course, that's when the fucking snow started to fall.

I watched it drift through the hole above in fat flakes. The ones that didn't cling to the walls coated the bodies in no time, and I knew I had to move, twenty feet or ten dug out. I gathered up my tools, slipping the bones into my belt, and started to climb.

Fifteen feet up, a foothold collapsed, banging my body against the wall. My ribs hammered into an exposed rock, and I hung there for a moment, gasping for breath, shoulders burning. When I thought I could go on, I pulled myself up and kept moving. The going was treacherous, the surface of the bones threatening to ice over as more snow fell.

At twenty feet, I was halfway between tiers. If the fall didn't kill me, the wait til spring would. I pulled the bones free with one hand, digging first one into the wall, then the other. I tested my weight, my stomach threatening to bottom out as I peered down. Not my brightest moment.

I found my spine and pulled myself up by one bone, then dislodged the other and plunged it ahead. One by one, foot by agonizing foot, I moved forward. My shoulders ached, then burned. I knew I was approaching failure at forty feet. I dug in again, and a mitten tore, exposing the raw flesh of my hand. I screamed as blisters burst, sending pus and blood across my handhold.

I slipped and grabbed for the bone, dislodging it. It fell for a moment that stretched into eternity, then clattered into a pile below.

"Fuck," I muttered.

I had ten feet to go and no way of knowing if I'd make it. I opened up a gate and reached for the dirt above me. The trickle was small, but enough. I augured holes and moved up them, one at a time.

Five feet. I felt something on the other side take notice. Three feet. The lip of the next tier was in sight. The Empyrean shuddered as the thing on the other side threw itself at my gate. I pushed back, sweat breaking out across my back and chest from the effort. One foot. The thing in the Empyrean screamed and I threw myself at the ledge, clearing it with my elbows. I snapped the gate shut as the horror on the other side hammered into it.

I panted from the exertion, hauling myself onto the tier.

The floor was about ten feet wide. To one side, a cell stood open. Inside was a filthy bed of straw and a honeypot. I rolled in and shut the door as quiet as possible. For a moment, all I heard was the hammer of my heart in my ears. The quiet of snow. And then the world winked out as exhaustion and relief caught up.

Nine

I slept in that hole for three days. Whatever was in the flesh and blood of the stalkers gave my body the fuel to heal. Not that we would have known. They were things of the Empyrean, so what magic resided in them was beyond any but the reach of the Callers.

I'd made it to the prison proper, and guards regularly patrolled the halls, making their way down a long spiral ramp letting off at each floor. When they passed, I did my best to scoop the filthy lice-ridden straw over myself until they were gone. I should have been a miserable itching mess, but whatever was in my blood now killed the little bastards, and they fell from me like hard pellets of snow.

I managed to eat whatever meager meals the guards dropped off. Mostly rotten meat and raw vegetables, but it was a damn sight better than decomposing flesh and blood. It wasn't until the fifth day I was discovered. The inmates at this level were little more than animals. When they saw signs of life in the cell, they meant to take and break the new meat.

Three of them came in the dead of night. They kicked the door in, meant to do violence. I showed them what violence was. Two, skinny as fenceposts, grabbed my ankles, spread my legs. A third, big as a house, came in, a wicked curved knife in his hand. He meant to make me a eunuch. I'd seen it before. They couldn't deal with the feelings inside, so they mutilated their victims and justified it with rape.

I kicked one of the little ones in the face, his nose and eye socket shattering where the bootheel caught him. He reeled back, blood black in the moonlight streaming from his skull, a keening wail running from his lips.

The other I grabbed and ran forward at speed, ramming him onto the big man's knife. He grunted once and shit himself. I let him go, and the body's weight pulled the knife from the leader's hands.

I knew if I let up, there wouldn't be a second chance. He came at me, nearly breaking my neck with a haymaker. As it was, I felt a tooth break free, my jaw snapping hard to the side. I spat blood and tried to blink away stars.

He must've had the same idea, because he got me in a chokehold. I squirmed, feet drumming on the ground. His arm was the size of a tree trunk. His cock pressed against my rear, hard as a rock.

I stomped down once, hard on his instep, and when he howled in pain, tore into his arm with my teeth. Hot blood, rubbery flesh filled my mouth, and I shook my head like a dog, trying to tear the chunk free.

He flung me away, and I staggered against the wall. The big man came at me again, and I ducked, throwing a fist into his groin. He squealed and doubled over. I threw a rabbit punch at the back of his neck and grunted in satisfaction as I heard the vertebrae break.

A shock went through my fist, and pins and needled followed. The big man toppled, and I pressed my bootheel into his neck until he stopped wheezing.

When it was over, I sank to the floor of the cell and nursed my broken hand. It ached in purple waves and was already swelling. I cursed. If it weren't one thing, it was another. I was safe for the moment, but come morning rounds, the guards would know there was an extra inmate down here, and he'd killed three men already. The best I could hope for if they caught me was a quick trip to the gallows.

I bound my hand best I could with strips from the mens' clothing, until I felt I could use it as a crude mitten and retrieved the big man's knife. Then I dragged their bodies one by one to the edge of the tier. I rolled them over the edge, soft thumps accompanying the end of each fall. When it was done, I kicked dirt over the worst of the blood and arranged the cell til it looked like no one had occupied it.

I wandered down the tier until I found their cells. I thought briefly about taking the big man's. He'd collected a lot of contraband, and it might be worth sorting through. But I knew the guards weren't entirely stupid. Seeing someone my size in his place would set them off.

I dug through his possessions and found a matchlighter and another curved knife. Then I took one of the skinny mens' cells. There was a stuffed mattress made from shirts and a passable pillow. I pulled the door shut and laid with my back to it. Hopefully the guards would assume I was too tired out from the big man's attentions to make much of a fuss.

Fallon was six when he found the matchlighter. I'd caught him out back, setting fire to little piles of twigs and leaves. It took a lot not to whip the boy as my father would've done to me. Instead, I took a breath, and sat beside him, watching the flame devour the fuel.

"What're you up to?" I asked.

He looked up at me, fear and a sort of pride warring within him. He'd made this, after all.

"Pretty, Pa," he said.

"Yeah. You know not to touch it though, right?"

"Why?"

"Well, just because something's pretty doesn't mean it can't hurt you."

"Like snakes?"

"Yeah, like snakes. And sometimes, if you don't watch those things, they get out of control and they hurt others."

"Like the Church hurt you."

"Yeah, buddy. Like that."

We were silent for a moment, watching the flame. Finally, he doused it with a handful of dirt. He stood to go, then paused. His face screwed up. I could tell he was thinking a Big Thought.

"Is Ma like fire?" he asked.

I laughed. "Yeah, Ma's like fire. But don't you tell her I said that." I gave him a wink, and he tried to return it, both eyes closing. I laughed again, and he scurried into the house.

I stayed, watching wisps of smoke rise from the leaves. Ginny startled me when she sat. I'd been in my own world.

"I'm like fire, am I Wil Cutter?"

I gave her a grin. "Hot as hell and dangerous when you're mad? Yeah."

"I'll show you dangerous."

She smacked me with the cloth in her hand, and I fell back laughing. She pounced, pinning me with her knees, then slapped at me playfully until I roared laughter, tears streaming from my eyes.

When I woke, the memory tattered, but the tears remained.

Guards came around twice that day, and I watched them make their rounds, heavy steps on the ramp as they went down, then up. They delivered us food, and I finished it. My hand throbbed like a bastard, though I already had feeling back in my fingers. I silently thanked whatever was in that stalker flesh. The small miracle of health it had granted me was a boon I couldn't have bought from the best sawbones on the plains.

The few inmates on this level made it habit to avoid me. They didn't know what happened, just that the big man who'd run the tier was gone, along with his two lackeys, and I was still breathing and living in their rooms.

I breathed another thanks to whatever gods would hear it from a damned man. I'd been spending most of my time tight as a clenched fist, so the little bit of leeway I'd bought had given me time to think and plan.

What did I want, anyway? If I got free, what did I plan? Did I want to go to war again? I shook my head, as if someone else had asked it. No, I'd seen too much of that. Too much of what happened during and after. Death and disease followed, and no one won. But I did want—I thought I wanted—revenge. You couldn't just burn a man's life down and expect to walk away. I owed Fletcher blood, and meant to have it.

When the guards made their last pass for the night, I stepped from the cell and looked up the tiers. Three more rose above me, fifty feet away from the next. The pit was over three hundred feet deep. I glanced over at the ramp. No one kept sentinel for the moment. Then I tested the Empyrean. It was stronger here, at night. Whatever kept my gift at a minimum was weaker. Likely two Nulls working in shifts. I wondered if one was Fletcher.

I turned my attention back to the ramp. A wooden boardwalk spiraling through the upper levels to the surface, the guards stuck almost exclusively to it, aside from food delivery and the occasional head-busting. At times, a Cleric clattered down the boards and offered some dying soul last rites. Whether they thought we deserved them or not wasn't in their canon. I suspected they only cared about paying lip service to their scriptures.

Still, guards were guards, and they were paid to keep the peace. And if you wanted their attention, you disturbed the peace. I knew what I'd have to do if I wanted out of this human honeypot. I walked back to my cell and shut the door, then curled up on the mat. It'd have to be at night, and I'd have to be rested.

Ten

Time passed. I only knew from the shifting of shadow to light on the walls of the Pit.

I got to know the old man in the cell beside me. He'd been lead down a week before, and mostly kept to himself. Still, he reminded me of Kent in a way. Grizzled, tired, unwilling to deal with a lot of shit. It was work, finding another human to connect with. I'd given that up when my boys went.

I went to his cell with my tray of food. I'd been eating well and could stand to miss a meal. I knocked and pushed his door open. He sat up, rheumy eyes searching the dim confines of the pit.

"Whozzat?" He asked.

"Just Wil," I said. "Next door. Just wondering if you'd like a little extra food."

He squinted, craned his neck. "Yeah? What're you up to?"

I set the tray down and backed away. "Just makin' friends. It's lonely down here."

The old man crouched, reaching a tentative hand out. When I didn't grab him, he lifted the tray and took it back to his mattress. He tucked in, devouring the scraps of bread and bruised apple.

"What you want?" He asked. "Ain't a thing a man does in here without wanting sommat."

"Mebbe I just want someone to talk to," I said.

I lowered myself into his doorway with a groan. He watched, chewing thoughtfully. He swallowed.

"You the one what done for Dolan and his boys?"

"Dolan?"

"Big man. Two nutless wonders with him."

I nodded. "Yeah, I did that."

"Good work that." He shoveled another chunk of bread into his mouth, took a sip from the tin mug. "So, what you want?"

I spread my hands. "A man can't do something like that without making a name. Was hoping for someone to watch my back."

"Aye, oh aye. Tell you what—you bring me food; I'll keep an eye out."

"That make you more comfortable?" I asked.

"Aye, more comfortable than chewin' on yer root. What you want me to watch out for?"

"Let me know when the guards are headed back up the ramp tonight."

"That all?"

I stood. "Yeah, that's all."

"You want a signal?"

"Just three whistles. You do that?"

He puckered his lips around the three teeth he owned and let out a short sharp whistle. He grinned. "Good enough?"

"Aye, good enough. Remember, tonight."

He nodded and went back to cleaning the tray. I made a slow circuit of the tier, checking the other cells. This must've been used as an overflow ring. Aside from me and the old man, only two other inmates lived on our tier, and they lay on their bunks, snoring blissfully. I marked the distance from my cell to the nearest, and from his cell to the ramp—it was the closest—then walked back to my bunk. I laid with my hands behind my head, looking up at the earthen roof.

Beetles, millipedes, and other insects crawled in and out, sending small rivulets of dirt raining down. I practiced opening gates and killing them in quick, precise strikes. Their bodies fell like pebbles, littering the floor. I tested my other theory then. I flicked the matchlighter, and opened a gate, grabbing the flame and shoving it to the other end. For a moment, the Empyrean resisted, then it was sucked in. It manifested on the other end, scorching a beetle the size of my thumb to a black husk.

I closed the gate and tucked the lighter away, then shut my eyes. It was only a few hours to dark, and I needed to be ready. My hand was nearly healed, but I'd need all the rest I could get.

Kent had a saying that became increasingly relevant as the war wore on and we found ourselves living in foxholes and hiding in the trees. *The hunters will tire.* It wasn't exactly deep or pithy, but it was a sort of optimism. The idea that the men we'd set ourselves against would eventually grow lax, complacent. I didn't put much stock in it then, facing the might of the Church. But now the Church was broken, and the shards they held together with threat and cash meant that same dogged determination was little more than window dressing.

You push a man who's just doing a job for a paycheck long and hard enough, he's gonna decide one day that it's not worth it anymore. What worth does a man put on his life, anyway? A hundred coins? A thousand? I didn't know the sum total of humanity, but I bet it was worth less than they'd admit. Everyone wants to live, no one wants to die.

The Church understood. They knew what a man really needed was a *cause*. Something to believe in. A fire in his belly worth braving the blades and bullets. True believers were few and far between. Kent was one. Fletcher another. Or at least I thought he was. Maybe he'd just changed what he believed in. Maybe the Church had offered more than amnesty. A way to save his soul, a new path in their dogma.

Regardless, men like that were dangerous. They *believed*. They believed in their heart and soul, fervently and wholly. Demagogues for a new age. The Church had learned to pivot. When the war ended, they turned their hand from conquest to law-keeping. I didn't know what they did these days in the capitol, it'd been silent so long, separated from the rest of us by the Waste our gates had made. If I had to guess, they were planning, looking to reclaim lost glory. No one had told them glory was dead.

Night fell, and the guards came round. I sensed the little bits and bobs on them that had touched the Empyrean. A pistol here, a knife there. One man carried a rabbit's foot. Another, the ear of a sow. Even before the war, those Callers with some small talent would enchant minor items, sometimes just giving them a glow, telling a soldier that it'd bring him luck, or protection from harm, or fortune. Most were lies at best, predatory at worst. I watched their lights bob by, first down the tier, pausing at each door for a head count.

I'd been fortunate. They hadn't cottoned to my deception yet. But then, they weren't paid to care what happened to the missing men. Arrogance made them assume death over escape, and that suited me fine. Light played on the walls of the cell as the guard stopped. He called out, as he did every night.

"Smith, show me you're alive!"

I shot my middle finger up, and the guard chuckled and moved on. I listened as they went from door to door, repeating the same check. It took only a couple minutes with just four of us on the floor. They started back up the ramp, heels making hard sounds in the night. Three soft whistles alerted me they'd moved on, and I tucked the matchlighter and the curved blades into my belt.

I moved to the old man's cell, stood before the door. I took a breath. Sometimes a man's got to do hard things. Things that tear away pieces of his humanity the way a dog rips flesh from bone. I took a breath and thought of my boys. Then I kicked in the door.

The old man shrunk against the wall. He was already shouting, one hand over his eyes, mouth working in terror. I lunged across the space and rammed a blade into his gut. He screamed in pain, and I dragged him from the cell, steel still in his belly as he kicked and thrashed. I threw him at the base of the ramp.

The other inmates, suddenly awake and aware, stood behind their doors, eyes wide as saucers. I paced to the closest and kicked it into his face, and he reeled back. He was small, and I grabbed him by the hair, dragging him beside the old man as he blubbered and wept. I let him go, and he rolled to his belly, scrambling to get away. I dropped onto his back and slammed the second blade into the back of his knee. It tore through flesh and cartilage, and the cartilage gave with a pop. The blade exited the front, and he screamed as it held him pinned to the earthen floor.

A commotion up top caught my attention, and I saw the guards coming back down, weapons drawn. I ripped the blade down the skinny man's leg, opening the back of his calf, blood gushing as he split like overripe fruit. His screams reached a crescendo. The tramp of booted feet—must've been about fifty of them on that ramp—and the shouting of voices for light so the gunmen could see what was going on followed.

"You want light?" I roared.

I opened a gate and fired the matchlighter. Then I pushed the flame to a hundred points—rope supports, aging boards—and fanned it. The bridge went up. Men stopped descending and started to scramble back up. So I lit the top as well. They were trapped, flames eating the ramp.

Some began to jump to the nearest tiers, terror giving

them strength. The inmates saw the opportunity, and charged from their cells, falling on the wounded and frightened guards. More screams and indiscriminate gunfire filled the air.

The inmates started to find guns—ones the guards on the ramp had been carrying and organized a counterfire. Bodies dropped in the firelight, falling into the depths. Below, the faintly glowing stalkers were back, and yet more screams of terror filled the air as they found new prey.

I knelt beside the two men I'd wounded. The skinny man was dead already. Blood loss had done for him. The old man breathed shallowly, hands around the knife in his guts. I pulled the blade from the other man, pressed it against the old-timer's wattle of skin beneath his chin, and slit his throat.

"Forgive," I whispered. I knew it was pointless. There was no forgiveness for the things I'd done.

A great noise pulled my attention. Callers rained o lightning into the prison, killing inmate and guard alike. Here I could be useful. I reached out and Nulled them. It took only moments for the inmates to regroup and shoot them down.

The prison was an abattoir. Then the ramp gave way with a groan like an ancient tree falling, dumping the remaining guards into the pit. They screamed on the way down. Some were smashed to bits. Others engulfed in flame. The smells of burning hair and cooked pork filled the air alongside woodsmoke. The sounds of agony and misery followed, hanging in the air alongside smoke and dust and snow.

Finally, it quieted but for the occasional cry of the

wounded or dying. I looked at the thing I'd done, then retrieved my blades, and started to climb the wall.

It took me an hour to climb to the next tier. If I wasn't welcomed as a savior, I wasn't unwelcome. I also wasn't the only inmate who'd had a hankering to be free. It took us two days to build a scaffold from the ruins of the ramp, and in short order, we were out into the world. The guards had abandoned the camp. It was white and cold, but it was ours. And fresh air'd never smelled so good.

The damned Church had taken the horses, though what supplies they'd run with had been only what they could carry, and there were great stores in a nearby warehouse. We ate like kings, found warm clothing, and more than a few guns. It felt right, having iron on my hip again, and I slept well for the first time in a month. If the boys or Ginny chose to haunt me that particular night, I took no notice.

We hunkered down for the winter, waiting for what we were sure would be a retaliatory strike. I dug myself a bunk between sacks of barley and oats and spent my nights there. It was quiet, for the most part. Most of the other men had taken the barracks. I found I craved solitude. When morbidity struck me, I found myself thinking again of Ginny.

Our first winter had been a hard one. The boys were a year or two off, I hadn't turned the field yet, and I still had a bit of wild in me. She caught me pacing on a day flurries whitewashed the windows. Finally, she let out an exasperated sigh.

"Sit down before you wear a hole in the floor," she said.

I paused. "Goin' stir crazy in here. Man's got to have somethin' to occupy him." I leered over at her.

"Cool your loins. I'm gonna have friction burn the rate you're going."

I started pacing again.

"Oh, for the love of—" she muttered. I heard the rustle of paper. "Come sit," she said.

I looked over, and she patted the seat of my chair. I wandered over, and sank into it, looked into her lap. She held a small book.

"You ain't got to look like a man going to his hanging. We're just gonna have a story," she said. "Stoke that fire. I'd like to feel my feet."

I threw a log on and poked the embers with an iron until it was crackling cheerfully, then settled back into my chair.

"Anyone read you stories before?" She asked.

I shook my head. "My Pa was too busy making sure I watched the cattle, or cleaned the hearth, or..." I trailed off.

She nodded and opened the book. "That man's lucky he ain't still around, or I'd tan his hide myself. Now just listen."

She began to read, her voice strong and clear, her cadence practiced.

"Billy Munsen walked into the old bruja's tent and breathed an involuntary sigh of relief. He'd been riding for three days, the path out of Hope little more than a dried rut in the desert hardpan. It was hot out there—had to be 100 in the shade, were there any shade that wasn't thrown by oven-hot mesas—hot enough for him to worry about the roan he'd ridden making the journey. He could hear it outside, whickering softly to itself as it took long draughts from the oasis. The caballeros in the other tents were nice enough not to snicker when he rode in, but he knew how he must look. Sixteen, raw, and pink and sweating like a dollar whore on penny night.

He stood in the relative cool of the dim tent and pulled out his wallet. He checked inside—10 dollars—a fortune for a family like his. He knew he'd need some of it to refill his saddlebags with food (water he could get from the pool in the oasis), and most of it for the bruja and her medicine. He slipped the wallet back into his shirt and let it hang from the thong around his neck. The leather was cool against his skin. It made him think of his mother, cold and pale in her bed, the sickness inside her long past fever. You could see it in the way her eyes were sunken, and her skin hung from her cheeks like grey curtains; the disease eating her from the inside out.

A voice from deeper in the tent came to him, scratchy and inflected.

"Hola, nino. You rode a long way on el camino muerto. Have a seat."

Billy stepped forward and found the back of the tent was dimly lit with a stumpy candle in a small metal holder. It lit the face of an old woman wearing a long purple dress and flowered scarf. Her skin was the color of old oak, and her face lined like the bed of a creek after a summer with no rain. She smiled, showing yellowed teeth, rheumy eyes crinkling at the corners, crazing her skin as though an earthquake had passed through the hardpan. She gestured at the chair across the small table from her.

"Sit. Sentarse."

Billy pulled out the chair and sat, the wood creaking under him. He shifted a little, the hard wood making the blisters on his flanks sting. He winced, and tried to hide it, afraid the old woman would think him too small or weak for his task. She continued to smile, as though she hadn't seen a thing. He pulled a kerchief from his back pocket and wiped the sweat from his forehead.

When she seemed sure he was settled, the old woman let the smile fade from her face in dips and drabs. Billy tried not to be scared. He knew the old fools in the village whispered the word bruja like it was a snake that would rear back and bite them. She was no such thing to most—just an old woman who knew medicine. Those who said that she was evil, or poison, earned those things, he felt. Despite his fear, more a fear for his mother than of this woman, Billy wasn't one of them. She looked at him, a squint creasing her brow, turning it into a fleshy bluff over her eyes.

"What's your name, nino?"

"Billy."

She nodded. "Si. Billy, you come to me for medicine for your madre?"

Billy nodded back. The lump in his throat felt the size of a boulder. He watched the old woman stand and totter to a corner of the tent. There was another table there, with shelves attached to the top. She rummaged around, the clink of glass on glass and the crinkle of butcher's paper filling the space. After a moment, she muttered something under her breath, and returned, a small glass vial in her hand. Its contents were silvery and slick, and seemed to move with a life all their own. She placed it on the table and sat back down.

"How much?" Billy asked.

The old woman weighed him. He thought of his mother, and the sweat that made the sheets cling to her pale skin, and the way she shook despite the heat radiating from her. He thought of her cough, and the moments when fever lit in her eyes, pale fire forcing foul words and moans of pain from her chapped lips. He knew the old woman could ask anything of him—five dollars, or his soul, and he would gladly pay either, and yet she did not.

"One dollar."

Confusion crossed his face, followed by a flood of relief when he picked his wallet from inside his shirt and fished out a dollar. He laid it on the table and closed his hand around the bottle, the glass cool in his palm. He drew it to him and watched the old bruja to see if she changed her mind. When she did not, he let a breath he hadn't been aware he was holding and held the bottle a little tighter.

The old woman smiled at him. "Go. Vaminos. Ride well."

Billy left; the bottle clutched to his chest. Behind him, the old woman hummed to herself.

The trail was hot as ever, and Billy rode with his hat pulled low and his shoulders hunched, as though it would somehow deflect the fire in the sky from cooking him in the saddle. His legs hurt, and his body ached. He was on the second day of his journey back, and he'd found the hardpan no less forgiving than it had been on the way out.

Fortunately, the caballeros had been willing to part with enough salted beef and bread to keep him through the trip, though he preferred to eat at night, when the desert was cool, and the dry food didn't pull the moisture from his lips like a cactus drew blood. He rubbed at his eyes and thought of the ranch, and his mother there, and hoped Ramon was keeping up with the chores.

He rode on for a time in near silence, his thoughts circling like buzzards over a carcass. The sounds of the roan's hooves clipping against the desert floor were loud amid the occasional scuttle and slither of snakes and lizards. Here and there cottonwoods added to the noise when the day kicked up a hot breeze, but aside from those things, the trail was bright and lonesome.

Night fell like a cool sheet over the desert, and for the first time, Billy looked up. Above, stars lit the whole of the sky, cold and distant perfect points of light in a velvet setting. They formed clouds and constellations and whorls, God's fingerprint hovering above the hardpan. It made him feel small, a sky like that, and though the sand hadn't cooled yet, and the breeze hadn't begun, Billy shivered a little—his mother would have said a goose walked over his grave.

He clucked softly to the roan, and she slowed, then stopped. Billy dismounted and led her to the side of the trail, near a small mesa with a depression at its base. He dropped the lead, and the horse wandered a few feet off. After a few minutes of using a small tin plate to dig a pit, Billy found a small pile of sagebrush fetched up against the rock, and brought it back, building a small fire. He dropped his roll beside it, then sat against the stiff fabric while he chewed a strip of jerky and sipped from his canteen.

The dark closed in while he worked, black and sure of itself. The roan whickered from somewhere nearby, and the sound of a lizard or a prairie dog scuttling through the sand drifted through the dark. His heart trip-hammered a bit while the night drifted in, and he fought the urge to saddle back up and ride from here until dawn split the night. Instead, he forced himself to take small bites of the jerky, to chew it methodically, and to think of home.

He thought of his mother, before the disease wormed its way into her flesh, of the way she looked standing against the sun, scrub grasses blowing behind her, the fabric on the line snapping in the wind. She would shade her eyes and look out, calling to him where he was digging a fencepost, or watering the cattle, and he would look up to where she stood, haloed in the light. Times like that he thought of how it should have been his father she was waving to, his father the one who should have been planting the timbers for the fence or slopping the buckets in the troughs. Those days were gone though —William Munsen had rode down the trail and never come back, and left Billy the man. So it went.

He sighed and washed the last of the jerky down with a few sips from his canteen, banked the fire, and rolled into his bedroll. He closed his eyes, and let the image of the ranch, warm against the sun, cottonwoods blazing in the evening light, lull him to sleep.

Billy awoke to the sound of someone stirring the embers of his fire. His pulse leapt like a wolf after prey, and he swallowed hard, but managed to lie still, back to the fire. He cursed himself for not pulling the rifle he'd brought from its place next to the saddle before he laid down. He lay in the dark, taking deep breaths, trying to pretend to sleep and listen at the same time.

Heat flared against his back as the fire re-kindled and

threw shadows against the mesa in front of him. He looked up at the puppet-show there, black silhouettes stark on the orange rock—his, laying prone, and the stranger, sitting on a rock, a long stick in his hand. The fire flickered and Billy's heart skipped as their shadows writhed, and he thought for a moment the man's had become that of a giant raven, perched over him.

"Stop playing possum, boy. I know you're awake."

The sharp end of the stick poked him gently in the back, and he instinctively shied away from it even as he tried to hold his water. He rolled in the blanket and sat up, pushing himself back from the fire a foot or two. No need to give the man an easy target. He rubbed sleep from his eyes so he could see who it was that had commandeered his fire.

The man sitting across from him was old. Older, anyway. His face was the same color as that of the bruja, though from the sun, not nationality. Lines rode his skin like a roadmap of one of the bigger cities Billy had seen in his primers.

The man had blue eyes set above a straight nose, and full lips that looked almost swollen in the orange light. A black shirt and chinos clung to his skeletal frame, and a blood-red kerchief wrapped around his neck. He smiled, and Billy heard the roan whinny. He cast about for the rifle, hoping it had fallen from his pack, but it was nowhere on the ground.

"Looking for this?" The man asked. He held up the Imburleigh, its long barrel black in the firelight, the wood stock orange against the flames. He tossed it to Billy, who watched it land in the sand with a puff of dust. After a moment, the boy scrambled for the rifle, and had it seated against the crook of his shoulder.

"Who are you?" He asked.

The man stirred the fire. Sparks jumped from the sagebrush and drifted upward, to the stars.

"Just an old man."

"What do you want?" Billy flexed sleep-numb fingers and slipped one inside the trigger guard.

The man didn't seem to hear, and instead looked up at the stars. "I knew your pa, you know."

"Bull." Billy said.

"William Munsen. Forty. Rode off this way a few years ago. Good man. Good man."

The way he said good man made Billy think of teeth in the dark, and sharp knives.

"What do you want?" He asked again, a tremor slipping into his voice.

The man in black lowered his head so Billy could see his eyes. The fire was reflected in his pupils, setting them ablaze. Billy thought of hellfire and damnation, like Pastor Ree talked about on Sunday mornings, and wondered if this was the sort of thing sinners saw before their last moments on God's earth. He wondered if his mother would see this. He gripped the Imburleigh harder still, until his knuckles stood out white against pink flesh.

The man finally answered. "A trade. That medicine for your life. The old woman—she's feeble. Hell, she's probably already lying in bed, flies circling her like a day-old turd in the sun. Ramon's long gone, the silver in his grubby fists. The little shit's probably already drank it all up." He opened his palms in a conciliatory gesture. "Just the medicine boy. If you share, I'll let you walk. If not, I'll eat you. Legs first."

Billy didn't have to think about it. He squeezed the trigger. The noise was loud and vast in the night and his ears rang *as it echoed off the tower of stone. A cloud of smoke, smelling of cordite, puffed into the night. The man was knocked off his rock, his shirt billowing out with the impact.* Not looking to see if he was dead, Billy, his heart hammering like a parade was tromping through his chest, jumped on the roan, snatching up the reins and kicking her flanks. She jumped into action, hooves tearing great clods of hard sand and throwing them behind the duo as they gained speed and pounded their way across the desert.

They fled, the night slipping around them. Mesas and scrub blurred by while overhead the stars seemed to slip their moorings and slide past in the night sky. They rode like that for some time, the sound of hooves and the roan's heavy breathing covering Billy's own heart, before he was aware of another sound, a loud rustling like a lizard's claws scrabbling on the desert floor.

He cast a glance over his shoulder. The man in black followed, running on all fours, his jaw elongated, a great tongue lolling from his mouth amid long needle-like teeth. Billy kicked the roan again, and they surged forward.

Behind him, another sound. The man had begun to sing.

"Them bones them bones them dry bones! Eat 'em up suck the marrow! Little boys and old women, simple men and fools, eat 'em up, suck the marrow! Them bones them bones them dry-y-y-y bones!"

Billy spurred the roan one last time, and they flew through the night. He felt flecks of foam on her flanks, and though he worried for her, his fear was greater. He would ride her until she fell, and then he would run until his feet bled, but he would not end a meal for the thing behind him.

They pounded on into the night, the vision of the thing

behind spurring them on. After a time, Billy no longer heard the man singing, though he did not dare slow their pace. Eventually, dawn broke the sky, pale and hot, and the roan slowed. He felt her heart hammering through her ribs, her labored breathing. She stumbled, and stopped, and he leapt from her in time for her to fall to her knees.

A part of him died inside seeing her like that, but he had no time. He dug into the saddle bag and grabbed the medicine. He stuffed it into his waistband and did the only thing he knew. He ran. He didn't know if the man was still chasing him, but he wouldn't be caught on his knees.

A mile down the road, he heard the horse scream. He ran on. He ran until his side threatened to split, and black spots flickered into his vision like flies fat from decay.

Still he ran.

Later, with the sun hot in the sky, and his feet bloody and blistered, the ranch came into view. He burst through the gate and into the house. Raul was there, wiping sweat from his mother's forehead, and for a moment, all he could feel was relief. The man in black was a liar. He gave Raul the medicine, who brewed it into a tea and gave it to his mother.

When she came around for the first time, he didn't tell her about the roan or the bruja, or the man in black. Instead, he held her hand and smiled back at her. Eventually, she fell asleep, and he did too, deep by her side.

His dreams were not all pleasant, and he often thought of the old woman who helped his mother and wondered if she could help him. He knew she wouldn't though—that was the *nature of things—you could only be innocent once. She would shy away from him, as others did now. He'd been touched by something dark, and it clung to him like leprosy.*

After, when he woke in the small hours, days and weeks months and years from then, he wondered if he would always be running from the man in black, and if one day he would fall and not be able to continue."

When she finished, she closed the book. I gave her a hard look, trying to see what might be hiding in her eyes.

"Why the look, Cutter?"

"Because you're a lot darker than I'd taken you for, love. What would have possessed you to read something like that?"

She stood and sat on the edge of my chair. She was lovely in the firelight. She leaned in and kissed me on the forehead.

"Because I know you would outrun the Devil if your family needed you," she said.

I wrapped an arm around her and pulled her into the chair with me. We watched the fire together til it burnt to embers, and then I carried her to bed.

Eleven

When I woke the next morning, I didn't have a plan, but I had an idea. Sometimes that's all a man needs. The sun was bright and harsh on the snow, light splintering like glass on the white. I made my way to the bunkhouse, pulling the door open against the stiff wind that had sprung up, whipping drifts across the field and into the pit. I stepped into the warmth, loosening my bandana and jacket. Quiet fell on the room for a moment as they noted my entrance.

A solid man, tall and wide at the shoulders, a scar around his neck, stood and walked over, grasping my hand.

"Wil Cutter. About time," he said.

The room came back to life, chatter and laughter taking their places at the table once again. He led me to a table in the back, three seats around it. A woman, grizzled, hair white, skin ebony, sat there already. She tipped a bit of whiskey into a glass and pushed it toward the empty seat, the tall man taking one of his own. I sat and tilted the glass in their direction.

"Cheers, fellas." I downed the drink, and the woman poured another.

"I'm Bear," the tall man said. "This here's Ox."

I nodded to both. "I'm—"

"Wil Cutter. Yeah, we know. We knew who you was in the war. One of the Three."

I set my glass down. "You looking for trouble?" I asked.

My hand drifted toward the butt of my gun. These two might have been soldiers once, maybe even Rangers, but they had been in that hole for a while. Prison made a lot of things—pain, horror, isolation—but mostly it made hard men not afraid to make hard choices.

Bear shook his head. "Gods no. We saw what you did down there. We was hoping to join up."

I did slug the second glass of whiskey then. "Join up with what?"

"You're going after them, right?"

I looked hard at him, then Ox. "You'd think those who'd been that close to the Church would rather be in the other direction." I nodded at the scar around Bear's neck. "Tried to hang you once, yeah?"

As if pointing it out reminded him it was there, Bear rubbed at it. "Yeah. I'd think you'd understand that, then. Man hurts you, you want to do a little hurt back."

"And what about you?" I asked.

Ox just looked at me over pouring another glass of whiskey. She tipped the bottle up and opened her mouth, waggled the stump where her tongue had been.

"Got it," I said.

"So?" Bear asked.

I turned my attention on him. "So what? Ain't no rebellion happening here."

Bear looked around the room, at the men playing cards and bullshitting. There were a lot. My tier might have been nearly abandoned, but the others had been full, and now the barracks was wall-to-wall men. Their voices hung in the air like a low hum, laughter echoed off the walls. They were happy. Happy to be free, happy to be from under the thumb of the Church for even a short while. I wondered if I could take that from them.

"We ain't got horses," I said. "And the Church is gonna be back. You and I both know that."

"Ox knows where the horses are."

I looked over at the little woman. She nodded and grinned that soft smile people missing parts of their mouth make.

"Yeah? And what you gonna do about ammo and supplies?" I asked.

"Seems like there's a warehouse here," Bear said.

"You want us to get the horses. Bring them back."

Ox brought her hands up, made a few signs. Bear nodded.

"There's a Church corral not five miles from here. Got a whole herd," Bear said.

"And these men?" I asked. "They willing to die for your cause?"

Bear shook his head. "Not mine. But yours, maybe."

I couldn't fault his need to fight. I'd felt it before. Some of these other men likely had as well. But we'd lost. Granted, we lost on our terms, but we'd lost.

"You really think you could win this time?" I asked. "Deep down. Last time didn't go so well, as I recall."

Ox signed something, and Bear whistled, high and piercing. The barracks came to attention. Silence fell over the room.

"How many of you boys want to bloody the Church's nose?" He asked.

A cheer went up. Bear stood.

"And how many of you boys give half a shit if we got a chance or not?"

Another cheer. Bear was picking up steam.

"Way I see it, we got two choices. One, we can slink off with our tails between our legs," boos filled the room. "Or we can take as many of those bastards with us when we're sent screaming to hell!"

The room erupted into cheers and stamping boots. Bear sat down and tipped up his glass with a smile.

"I just handed you a powder keg. Just needs a match."

I looked at him for a long moment, drained my glass again. I set it on the table with a *thunk*.

"You're a bastard."

Ox grinned.

"The both of you."

"Aye," Bear said. "And then some."

I stood. "Get some rest. We got to get those horses before spring breaks."

"That's the spirit," Bear said.

"Remains to be seen how willing it'll be," I said, and stomped out the door.

I slept like the dead. And dreamt of them, too. Ginny'd come down with something. Croup, most likely. The boys hovered at the edge of the room, ghosts themselves. They were afraid of her fits, of the way her small frame wracked with the heave of her chest. Sweat covered her from head to toe, and she complained of being hot and cold, cold then hot. Her skin held a pallor shining with fever light.

The dream twisted, becoming something darker, and I watched in horror as she found her feet, staggered across the room. Her bare feet left wet marks on the floor; piss dribbled down the inside of her thighs as she walked.

The boys stepped from the shadows, and I saw their flesh, charred from fire, empty holes where their eyes had burst from the heat and run in streaks down their face. Their cheeks had been eaten away in holes; teeth yellow and cracked from the fire showed through. They opened their mouths and cried in pain, and smoke issued from between their lips.

Ginny gathered them up in her arms, holding them close. She kissed them atop their heads, the char there flaking away and staining her lips black. Then she turned jaundiced eyes on me as a crack opened in the earth. Fire gouted from within.

"This is on you, Wil. 'Tis is your work," she said.

She leapt into the crack, screaming on the way down as the fires devoured her whole. I wept and screamed and pleaded, and when the dream ended, woke in a cold sweat. The warehouse was silent. Water dripped from the eaves as the first warm winds of spring threatened to break on us. Somewhere nearby, a barn owl let out a hoot. I fell back onto the grain sacks and closed my eyes.

No more dreams came that night. I think if they had, I would've eaten a bullet then.

Morning broke, and I felt like I was swimming upward in molasses. Fortunately, someone had found coffee and brought me a steaming cup and a bowl of oats. I managed both and made my way over to the barracks. The men were unruly as ever, but Bear and Ox were already waiting. They'd found heavier coats and bandanas as well to keep the cold air out. Bear carried a pistol the size of a small cannon on his hip, and Ox an axe that wouldn't have been out of place in a woodsman's shed. Two more hatchets hung from her belt. I nodded at them.

"Likes to cut, does she?"

Bear chuckled. "I gave up that argument a long time ago."

I checked my own weapons—the two curved blades and a pistol I'd liberated from the stores.

"Ready?" I asked.

Ox shouldered an oversize pack and signed something.

"Horses are about four, five miles north."

More signing.

"Says they don't keep much guard. Usually, two men with the rancher and his hands."

"How's she know all this?" I asked.

"Guards were chatty. Liked to talk about their mounts.

Turns out when someone can't interrupt, people will go on for hours."

We stepped into the morning. Sun lay thick on the snow, dazzling and warm. Spring wasn't far away. I wouldn't be sad to be rid of this place. Not just because of the Church likely coming back as soon as the trails were clear, but because the pit was going to start to stink. On top of the bodies, we'd been emptying our honeypots into it. It was going to attract all manner of unpleasant critter.

I squinted as we passed it. Already, a light shimmer rose from the opening. Another few days, a week or two, and it'd be a full-blown deadland. The Church'd never be able to use it again. I chalked it up as our first victory, and worth the cost. The Pit had made more monsters than not. And not just out of the men jailed there.

Bear caught me looking. "Nostalgia?" He asked.

I shook my head and pointed out the mirage lines. He whistled low.

"Helluva thing, seeing one born."

"Yeah, it is at that."

We moved on, around the buildings making up the camp and through the gate. Ox led us on a small switchback until we were headed north again. The snow was shin deep. The three of us left a trail a blind badger could follow, but it couldn't be helped. Coming back, we'd sound like thunder. I just hoped luck would hold out before the first of the Church scouts started poking around.

We ate on the way, jerky and water, bits of hard cheese. We'd agreed not to stop unless someone was injured, or we ran into trouble, and made good time. The sun rose high, and water dripped from the trees. The whole world smelled fresh, like it'd been scrubbed clean by winter.

I was lost in my thoughts, the landscape and time passing by, when I saw the tree. Gnarled and twisted, the branches barely clung to life. I wandered away from our little group, making my way over. Bear called out, but I didn't stop until I was at the trunk, running my hand over the letters carved there. Memory poured over me, and I closed my eyes for a moment.

Kruger and Benton, sweating in the cool air. A tearing feeling as we ripped reality apart. The sanity-shattering thing hauling itself from the gate, taking no heed of the little life at its feet when greater sustenance filled the plains. The path of shimmering hate it left in its wake as it decimated the enemy, heading east, toward the sea. Toward Elan.

I head Bear and Ox coming. They halted just behind me.

"You okay?" Bear asked.

I nodded and turned away from the tree.

Bear stumped over, leaned in. He peered at the letters we'd carved, the bark peeling away. Then he turned back.

"It was here."

I nodded. The three of us had carved our initials on the tree, just before we opened the gate and let the thing on the other side through. Maybe we'd meant it to be a monument to our victory over the Church. Maybe we'd just hoped someone would remember us, even if it was only the trees.

I started off on the northerly path again, and the other two followed. Bear pulled alongside me.

"Why'd you agree to this?" He asked.

"Agree to what?" I asked.

"This. Taking on those boys—us—the cause?"

I looked up. A hawk wheeled overhead. As I watched, it dove into the trees, disappearing for a moment.

"Ain't no cause. Just a man to kill."

The hawk burst from the canopy, something small and brown clutched in its talons. I looked over to Bear.

"Why'd you want to follow a man like me, anyway?" I asked.

Ox gestured back at the tree, signed. Bear nodded. "You did something great once."

"Was it?"

"Was it what?"

"Great."

"Aye, and we think you could do more."

"Un-huh. And if'n I don't?"

"Don't what?"

"Agree."

Bear shrugged. "It'll still be a hell of a ride."

I snorted in amusement and let it drop. They were wrong, even I knew that much. We'd shattered the Church, but the land suffered. I often thought about Farson's belief in the world moving on, and thought I understood it now. This world was dying, in slow measure, but dying nonetheless. I wondered if maybe he'd been a prophet, because then, all we'd wanted was change. And that's what we got, at my hands, for better or worse.

We reached the edge of the tree line. Just past the shelter of limbs, the sunlight gained in strength, dazzling our eyes. It took a minute to blink away the sunspots. A field of unbroken snow lay before us, the ranch at the far end, nestled in the leeside of a tall foothill. The mountains loomed closer, throwing one another into shadow like jealous siblings.

Horses milled in the corral, breath misting in the morning breeze. A trainer was out with them, running them on leads, while two guards with long rifles paced the perimeter.

"Long way up. No cover," Bear said.

I looked at the tree line, extending left and right. The Church had done a good job keeping lines of sight clear. What we needed was a good blowing snow. Or a distraction. I looked again at the tree line, took a few steps back in. I knew the lay of this land. A hillock here, where roots protruded like a crown. A pine with branches so low the snow had never penetrated.

"Got an idea," I said.

I put Bear behind the hillock, a length of rope running across an overhead limb. Its end was tied in a loose noose. Ox I had scramble under the pine, axes out. When they were hidden to my satisfaction, I pulled my pistol and walked free of the trees. The guards at the ranch had come around again, and I took two shots in their direction. I didn't have hope of hitting them at this range, but I meant to get their attention. It did the trick.

I'd sent an unmistakable cloud of smoke up to mark my location. Sharp whistles echoed across the prairie, and the men found their mounts in seconds, riding hard, rifles leveled across their forearms. I waited until they were headed my way and bolted for the trees. Bullets smacked into the trunks, making sounds like angry wasps as they buzzed by. Goddamn rifles. I'd nearly forgotten the range on the blasted things.

I reloaded and fired a couple more rounds from behind cover to really rile them up, then dove into a stand of juniper and hawthorn. The thorns were wicked, but they bothered me little with the thick hide jacket I wore. The sound of hoofbeats drew near, and I held my breath. The riders slowed to enter the forest. I crawled from the stand of bushes to a dry creek bed, then threw a stone in their direction.

They spurred their horses, galloping carelessly through the copse. A sudden snapping sound, and a riderless horse flew past me. I peered from around a tree. Bear had got his man, the guard dangling from the noose, neck twisted at an odd angle.

The second screamed a moment later as Ox launched herself from the pine, burying both hatchets in the man's back. He made a wet gurgling sound, like a broken teakettle, and fell from the saddle.

And like that, we were done. Bear and Ox sat one saddle, and I the other. We rode to the ranch. Not a lot to tell after that. Ranch hands aren't built for war. We killed them quick, which was the mercy we could afford, and ate a good meal from their larder after.

Later, as the sun set, we went outside, and there waiting for us, were the other men from the prison. I looked over at Bear. He shrugged.

"How'd you expect to get all these horses out of here?" He asked.

I laughed and saddled up. We rode back to the prison one last time, this time taking the road. Five miles is nothing on a good horse, and these were the best.

We divided the men up. Not everyone could ride, so we gave them the hard jobs—cooks and quartermaster, farrier and washer. You'd think soldiering was hard, but experience told me it took less brain and effort to pull a trigger than it did to feed a thousand men. The ones who could fight, but not ride well, we made dragoons. And the rest were our cavalry. One thousand men total, give or take. Five hundred cavalry. Four hundred dragoons. And the rest logistics. We loaded the camp wagons with supplies, the sun setting fully behind the hills.

Bear rode up beside me. I'd given him charge of the cavalry, Ox the dragoons. He held something long and bright in his hand and presented it to me. I took it, felt its weight. I hadn't held a cavalry saber in years. It still felt right.

"Where to?" He asked.

"East, I think," I said.

The capitol lay that way. And if I had my guess, Fletcher had already set out for it, hoping to drum up reinforcements. Bear wheeled his horse and called out commands, and soon we were on our way, riding into the night.

Twelve

We rode through the night, trying to make time. The snow had begun to melt in earnest, making a muddy wreck of the track we followed. There were a few towns along the way to the capitol, and I suspect Fletcher would try to raise levies from each before moving on. Chorn and Coldharbor lay directly on the road we traveled. Beyond that, the highway broke and crumbled to dust in the Waste, the aftermath of the thing we'd called through the gate. Beyond the Waste lay pastoral fields and the sea. And there, at the mouth of three rivers, sat Elan, seat of the Church.

I would have preferred not to ride through the Waste. I suspected the men felt the same. It was wrong there, twisted in ways that'd make a hale man sick. Stalkers were abundant there, as were other horrors. The Callers had tried to heal it, but whatever poison we'd unleashed had effectively cut it off from the rest of the world.

I suspected the Church preferred it that way. It was

easier to keep the savages away if the border killed them. At least to their way of thinking. And I imagined they enjoyed the ivory tower separation from the rest of the country. They'd always believed in the purity of their moral authority. Remaining untouched by the Waste only reinforced that in their thinking.

Over the years, they'd leveraged that isolation to add to their mystique. Rumors abounded of what lay on the other side. A new army, waiting to be unleashed on the plains, wiping out the Nulls once and for all. Foundries and manufactories to replace their lost technology. Strange machines to duplicate Null powers. The most frightening rumor was they wanted access to the destruction we wielded, and to that end, had enslaved hundreds of Nulls as a doomsday weapon.

Whatever the truth, I had no urge to go all the way to the capitol if it could be avoided. I wanted Fletcher. That was all. If I had to draw the whole Church out, or sacrifice every man with me, I'd do just that. The thought brought a wry smile to my lips as I recalled Ginny telling me that once I set my mind to something, you'd have better luck bleeding a stone than getting me to change my path.

We had three days to Chorn, a small burg on the Yellow River. It appeared overnight as we cleared the trees, emerging from where the forest curved to the south on a north-east bent. The water already cut through the thin ice covering its surface, and dirty snow clung to the banks, giving the whole of it a muddy appearance.

We kept ourselves between it and the mountains to the north, the foothills still small and infrequent. The land widened out as we went, the forest dropping away til we rode a gently rolling plain. Here, in full sight of the sun, the snow had melted but for the shadowy lees of larger hills. Small stands of maple and poplar dotted the landscape, though scrub brush and stunted grass were more common.

The sky was wide and blue before us, as if someone had lowered the heavens, and it hung overhead like a painted fresco. The sound of a thousand men on horseback was like thunder, even at a gentle canter, and the men were in good spirits. It felt like the whole of the world lay open for us to pick the meat clean. I listened to snatches of talk as we rode, idle conversation shared like wine between the men.

I thought of Kent, then. Of our days with the Free Blades. It was after the war, and they'd bought us out of the pit. They needed men, men who could do the hard work, the wet work. We didn't have a side back then. Maybe we were broken. But the cities hired the Blades because they needed protection. Protection from the Church and those pockets of Rangers who were running roughshod, trying to kill each other and anyone in their way.

I watched the countryside pass, picked up mirage lines indicating deadlands and led us around them. The things from the Empyrean—better not to have truck with them. I thought of another ride years ago when Kent and I had been assigned execution detail.

I listened to the creak of the boards on the wagon, and the stamp of the horses' hooves as they tramped through ruts made hard from an early frost. I watched my own horse blowing steamy breath through its nose, and felt its flanks shift under the saddle blanket, heat rising up into my thighs. The men arrayed around me rode easily, almost carefree, rifles laid across their laps. It was a lie any man would know looking at their faces. Hard eyes, set mouths. Yet even there, another lie, deeper. I looked at the trees, bare from a hard autumn, and sighed.

They kept a wide berth from me and the wagon. Respectful distance, some might call it. But I knew the truth. You didn't call a man like me to the wilderness unless a man was dying or destined to be so. I knew the names they called me under their breath. *Rook. Vulture. Rattlebones.* For them, it was bad luck of a sort. They'd made their peace with the land, since their gods hadn't yet, and to invite one of the outcasts was like letting a fox into a henhouse.

A crow flapped from a nearby branch, startling me in the saddle, and the appaloosa under me shied to one side. I took the reins in hand and brought her back to the path, but not before snorts of amusement from the posse reached my ears. I glanced over at the man in the wagon, glad at least there was another they had less of an opinion of than me. I glanced over at the prisoner, struggling with a moment of indecision, then steered my horse over, toward the man in the lead, lean with a wide-brimmed hat and a stern set to his mouth. A star sat on his chest, a symbol of his authority. I tilted my head as I came alongside.

"Bill," I said.

Bill nodded back. "Captain. How can I help you?"

I swallowed. I didn't feel up to the task—it had been a hard cold ride, and these were hard cold men. And frankly, I preferred the warm confines of the barracks in Redwood. I wondered sometimes if it had been duty or the stipend that called me to service, and whether I would have answered if someone told me I'd be ministering to the lowest in creation. Still, the good gods helped those who helped themselves, and hated a coward, platitude, cliché. I cleared my throat.

"I'd like to talk to the prisoner."

Bill grunted. "He lies."

"Everyone lies," I said. "He still deserves a chance to come clean before he stands at the feet of his gods."

Bill blew a breath out, white and misty in the morning air. "Be my guest, Captain. I'm just here to arrange the meeting."

I turned my horse, its hooves scuffling on the hard trail, and headed to the back of the procession. The sun hadn't quite broken the horizon, and night held to the early hours like a wolf worrying a bone. I nodded to Kent, driving the wagon, and passed by the clapboard sides. Frost rimed the wood, and the prisoner shivered a little, though from cold or circumstance, I couldn't be sure. It's a hard thing, knowing the time and place of your death, I imagined. Harder still knowing it was coming with the sun. I wheeled my mount around again and pulled into a steady trot beside the creaking wheels.

The man in the back of the wagon was thin and ragged, a wiry beard sprouting from a weak chin. A smell cut through the scents of warm horseflesh and hay as I drew close, and I wrinkled my nose despite an attempt to appear dignified. The man smelled of sweat and spoiled meat and blood, a sickly-sweet copper odor clinging to him. He was pale, blue veins peeking through here and there just below the surface of his white flesh. He lifted sunken eyes from behind wire-rim round glasses and gave me a mournful look. I shivered and thought it the look of a man who'd seen more than his mind could contain, and only wished for it to be stripped away like an undertaker removing offal from viscera.

I opened my mouth, intending to address the prisoner, and the wind picked up. It rattled the bare branches around them and sent leaves skittering across the trail, the sound like claws on wood. The prisoner cringed and raised his hands as if to ward off a blow, the chains that shackled him jingling as he did so. After a moment, when it was clear there was no blow or attack coming, the man lowered his chains and hung his head again.

The sudden movement sent my heart skipping, and I took a moment to calm myself, so my voice didn't waver. When my confidence returned—because who could say what this man was capable of—I cleared my throat, as if preparing to discuss the latest news from Copper Creek.

"You fear the wind, Mister—" I asked.

"Hart. And yes." Hart refused to meet his eyes, scanning the tree line.

"They caused the east wind to blow in the heavens. And by Their power They directed the south wind," I quoted.

"Is that supposed to make me feel better?" Hart asked.

I shrugged. "It's a reminder. Your gods control the wind. It's their hand that stirs the leaves on the bough, the face of the water. And where the gods go, there is nothing to fear."

Hart's eyes roved. Paused. Roved. He stared into the woods for a moment, and then turned to me. "I'm not sure They've made it out this way yet, Captain."

"Why is that, Mr. Hart? You know of course, the gods are in all things."

"Whose gods?"

I pursed my lips. "You seem to have struggled with this Mr. Hart." I looked ahead, at the path that wound into the woods and toward our inevitable destination. The track rose gently, leading us upwards. At its peak, a crooked finger of timber, and a rope, open to the sky.

Maybe they thought building it there would allow the gods' judgment to fall more easily on the guilty. Maybe it just kept the stink of the dead upwind. I shook myself. "You have limited time now, sir. Would you like to confess?"

"Confess?" Hart looked at me, contempt in his features I didn't understand. Did he believe himself innocent?

"No," Hart continued. "But I'll tell you a story."

I shrugged it off. "You're welcome to unburden yourself however makes you comfortable."

"Aye, maybe. What makes one man comfortable may be mighty uncomfortable for another, though."

He paused and took a breath, maybe tasting the air for the right moment. I hadn't expected theatricality from the man. Then again, what was one supposed to expect from the condemned? What did they have to lose? When I had begun to wonder if he was going to speak, Hart's voice broke the silence.

"My pappy came here 30 years ago, looking to stake a claim. This was all wilderness then. Not like this, but hard wilderness. Wild. He was from Alemani stock, though I wouldn't hold that against him. Not that it matters, but you've got to understand, those men, they were just trying to live. Some of them it made mean. Some a little crazy. He built a home about ten miles back—but you know that.

Anyway, it was important to him that we keep that house. Tradition, you ken?"

I nodded. The sheriff had sketched in some details.

"What happened to your father?" I asked.

Hart shrugged. "Consumption. Got him in the winter of '56. What the sawbones said, anyway."

"You didn't believe him?"

He shook his head. "Maybe at first. Maybe a little." He shrugged. "Maybe it was the sickness that got into him. *A sickness*, anyway."

"How do you mean?"

"Doesn't matter." He craned his neck over his shoulder, at the path they rode down. "It's done, and I'm not long for this world."

"Truth doesn't matter?"

Hart shook his head. "Truth, lies, what is and what might've been. None of it matters once it's done, does it? It's over, and you're left with the after. For as long as that lasts."

"Does that make you afraid?" I asked.

Hart looked at him, hard, and considered. "Maybe once. Now, I don't know. Part of me is going to be glad to quit this Earth."

"Because of what you've done?"

"Wasn't me, Captain. I told the sheriff and his men, and the judge, and I'll tell you—wasn't me. And even if it was, I don't recall. But what I do remember—I don't want it in my brain anymore."

"Who then?"

"You mean w*hat*."

"Pardon?"

"*What* is the word you're looking for."

"Tell me about it, then."

He took in a breath and let it out in a long plume. Hung his head, hair falling in lank locks over his eyes. He seemed to shrink in on himself. After a minute, he spoke.

"It was cold that night. You know the house is on a hill, in a clearing. Pappy set it there so he could see what was coming, Indian or beast, or both. The drawback there is that the wind can whip mighty mean 'round the eaves when it's got its back up. Sounds like a banshee when it's blowing hard. You know the banshee, Captain?"

I shook my head.

"Old Genn story. Say it's the ghost of a woman, and if you hear her scream, someone's gonna die. Maria, my wife—she's Gennish—that's where I learned of it. Least she was, before. Hard to be anything the way they found her." He paused for a moment, though whether for effect or to fight down the memory, I couldn't tell. Hart took a breath and went on. "Superstitious as hell. That wind would blow up, and she'd fork her fingers and spit through them. I used to laugh at her for that.

"'Just gettin' spit on the floor,' I'd tell her.

"The kids though, they'd take their momma serious. You know how it is, little 'uns and their mothers. They'd follow suit, and fork their fingers and spit too, though being kids, they'd just spit on their hands and end up wiping it on their jumpers.

"That night though, she didn't do it. Can't say why—maybe she was settling in finally, maybe she was just feeling comfortable. Anyway, that wind blew on, and she was too busy cookin' up dumplings, or a piece of venison, or summat, and the Devil's fork never occurred to her. "

He shook himself and went on.

"I was sitting by the fire. Had an old book my pappy had left—something by one of those pilgrims—and my pipe. Never lit it in the house though. Made things stink awful. Anyway, that wind was blowin', and I hear something coming through the trees, so I put my book down and get up, over to the door. I open it and the wind damn near blows it out of my hands, but I kept a good grip, and I looked out toward the tree line. Sure enough, something's moving down there—probably a deer or an elk—I can see the antlers, but we got enough meat for now, so I close the door and sit down.

"'What was that?' Maria asked me.

"'Just the wind,' I said."

He heaved a sigh. "Damn fool thing to say." Another sigh. "Anyway."

"Didn't think nothin' else about it until after dinner. Stomach was troubling me, you see. Felt like I was still hungry, but I couldn't account for it, so I thought *Hell, I'll go get that deer. We could always use the extra after all, and the air will do me good.* So, I got my rifle and walked down to the trees, but I couldn't see a thing.

"The wind kicked up, and was howling something fierce, but I thought I'd go a little further. Kept seeing those antlers, between the trees, so I kept going. Got to a clearing a few hundred yards from the house, and it's like that deer had just up and vanished. Not a track, not a trace. And the whole time I'm chasing it, all I could think of was how that stag would taste. Steak and stew and roast. By then I'd worked myself up into stomach pains.

"Then I heard the door banging in the wind, and thought I'd latched it. I headed back."

He looked up at me, and his face was pale. Tears stood in his eyes. His throat bobbed up and down, like a rabbit caught in a snare. For a moment, I thought the man was having a fit. We rode in silence for a time. Finally, Hart got a hold of himself, and managed to swallow. He heaved a deep sigh.

"Do I gotta go on?"

I shook my head, but said gently, "No. But it might do your soul some good."

Hart sniffed and rubbed at his eyes for a moment, then cleared his throat. He coughed, sniffed again, and then went on, plowing forward as if he saw the end barreling at him as the track rose up the hill.

"The house was open when I got back, and there was muddy tracks from the threshold, but they trailed off after a few yards. Smelled—smelled something fierce, too. But goddamn was I hungry by the time I got back.

"They was a mess—opened from groin to gullet, but by then, all I could feel was the pain in my stomach, and the sound—my God, it was a *roar* in my belly. I went from pantry to cupboard to stove, but there weren't a bite to eat, like someone had emptied every cabinet in that short time I'd been gone."

He broke down in sobs. I waited for him, gently administering *It's all right, sons* until the man calmed. When Hart recovered, the rest fell out of him as though he'd been opened up.

"I buh-buh-bit her. I bit off a big strip of her thigh, and my God, it tasted so good. And that wind died right down, and I finally found peace that night. I don't know how long I ate on her leg, that leg I'd caressed and kissed and admired, but when I looked up the first time, sated, some *thing* peered in the window. A deer skull atop a wasted body watching, and its eyes were pits of fire, its lips tattered and bloodstained. I don't recall the rest. Then the sheriff and his boys showed up."

His eyes were wide and his pupils pinpoints. One of the horses stepped on a branch, snapping it neatly in two, and I started. Hart snapped.

"OH GODS, IT'S HERE IT'S HERE IT'S HERE OH GOD—"

The sheriff appeared beside him and fetched him a blow to the side of the head, cutting the man's screams off. Hart's skull rocked to one side, and his eyes went sleepy. He fell quiet. Bill looked at me.

"Captain. I think you're done here."

I nodded, and with one last glance at the prisoner, we rode to the front of the line. We rode in silence for some time, the only sounds those of the horses and the wagon.

"Warned you."

"Did you see it?"

The sheriff didn't respond immediately. When he did, his voice was sober. "I served at Ulrich, you know. Twenty thousand dead. Men trying to hold their guts in, screaming on the field, nursing slowly rotting wounds. But this... this was different. *Evil*, Captain.

"His family was split, like he said. But that knife was in the basin. And his hands were red. Gore up to the elbows. Pan on the stove." He glanced back at Hart. "Men lie, Captain. Everyone lies. But this..." he trailed off, and when he didn't pick it back up, I asked the question that had slipped into my mind.

"Did you see the tracks he talked about?"

Bill nodded. "Hoofprints. Probably their pony got loose. We found it a day later, by the stream, half-eaten. Likely wolves."

"You don't believe there could be other possibilities, sheriff?"

Bill looked at me. "I do. Just not the kind of mumbo-jumbo you're talking about. No offense, pastor, but I've seen enough darkness in the world without needing your devil. There's enough evil in a man's heart. He doesn't need a boogeyman as an accomplice."

We rounded a curve on the hill, and the forest opened up. Trees fell away to expose a crossroads, the road traveling on to the cardinal points of the compass. The gallows stood beside the center, tall and skeletal against the lightening gray sky. From behind us, Hart whimpered. We rode until we were beside the killing tree, and dismounted, Bill and Kent pulling Hart from the back of the wagon.

Bill pulled a small black hood from his back pocket and pulled it roughly over Hart's head, the man coughing out a sob as it went. Despite his talk, I thought the end did not come as glibly as the words for some.

I retrieved the Rites from my saddlebag and walked the steps of the gallows, bootheels echoing on the boards, to stand by the lever. Bird droppings and leaves crunched underfoot as we came to a halt. They led the prisoner up the stairs, legs watery as he walked. More than once they had to brace his arms to keep him from falling down. Soft weeping came from inside the black fabric over his head.

On the platform, the sheriff looped the noose around Hart's neck and tightened it, then stood to the side. This was it, then. The time when confession turned to punishment. I read from the Rites.

"*Yea, though I walk through the valley of the shadow of death...*" My voice blended into the background as the wind kicked up.

The horses whinnied, and from somewhere in the forest, a branch broke. A flash of white between the trunks. A dark stain spread across Hart's trousers, the acrid smell of urine rising in the air. From inside the hood, he screamed himself raw.

"PULL THE LEVER PULL THE LEVER PULL THE—"

A creak and a thump as the mechanism tripped, the trapdoor slamming open. The clear *snap* of Hart's neck, the sound mirroring the breaking branch in the woods. The sharp odor of bowels evacuating. The creak of the weight of a body on a rope as it swung from the gantry.

The wind died down, and my voice carried on the clear air.

"*...deliver us from evil.*"

Hart's body spun gently. I closed the book and looked out at the woods. From somewhere in the gloom, light caught a set of bone-white antlers.

"Wil."

Bear's voice cut through the memory. I must've been sleeping with my eyes open because night had crept back around. We called a halt, the men setting up tents and campfires that lit the plain with bright spots of orange fire. I dismounted, one of the camp followers taking my mount—I'd named him Threader—and brushing him down. Bear and Ox joined me, and we fried a rasher of salt pork up with some winter potatoes.

When we'd finished eating, I lay back on my bedroll. My body had finally healed the last of its hurts, and I felt good for the first time in what felt like ages. Movement caught the corner of my eye, and I turned my head. Ox was signing something to Bear. The big man nodded.

"What's the plan, boss?" He asked. "We're getting close to Chorn. How you want to play this?"

I gave it a little thought. "Way I see it; we got a head start on Fletcher. He likely holed up in Chorn, raised a levy. Got stuck there though, with the snows. If we ride hard over the next couple days, I think we could catch him out."

"Yeah? You got an axe to grind with this Fletcher?"

I grunted, ignored the question. My business was my own.

"I want to split the men," I said.

"Why?"

"I want to take cavalry north, then split the troop and bend the second group back toward Chorn, hit them from behind. The dragoons can head straight on. Lollygag a little. When Fletcher sees them, he's gonna be spoilin' for a fight. Ox and his men draw him out, we fire the town, hit him from behind."

Bear nodded. "River to the south—he'll have to rout to the north."

"And I'll be waiting there."

Ox whistled, signed something again, fingers flying.

Bear nodded. "We'll cut them to ribbons. That's cunning."

He gave me a look of appraisal that said he approved. I didn't much care either way. I lay back and looked up at the stars, arms behind my head. I remembered Dumai, and my stead, and my gut clenched.

I was a long time getting to sleep.

Thirteen

Morning came too early, and still I was awake, ready. We took enough time to give every man and unit their orders, then I took my five hundred and moved north. We rode hard, hooves pounding the plain like war drums. The ground steadily rose, and when I felt I had a good view of the lay of the land, I split our forces again, sending half the riders south and east. In the clear dawn, our dragoons moved at a clip toward the rough shadow of Chorn, the Yellow River a coppery ribbon just beyond.

Someone once said war is a lot of waiting punctuated by sheer moments of terror. In my experience, it was probably one of those things that should be engraved in stone. Right next to the other truth about war: There's no one it doesn't touch.

The first volley of gunfire came from within Chorn, the sound little more than tinny pops in the air. Smoke rolled outward from between the buildings, a cloud between the town and the dragoons. Several fell, slumping from their saddles, others were dragged under as their horses went down. Screams filled the air.

The dragoons dismounted, returning fire in a crackling wave splintering and cracking wood from homes. More screams, and the men in town poured from the main street, Fletcher's own dragoons meeting mine. They moved in close, too close for guns, and blades came out.

Close work then, knife and sword and fist. Cutting and bleeding and screaming. Trailing guts and blood in the dirt. My cavalry hit the town from behind, and the torches lit, the first roofs going up. Black smoke followed, obscuring half the battlefield.

Men and women poured from the blazing homes, and the cavalry cut them down as they fled, sabers making short work of the runners. Fletcher's own cavalry, just emerging to bring the fight to the dragoons, wheeled around, and the men with long guns started firing.

I'd given them orders to disregard the men and kill the horses. It worked, Fletcher's cavalry breaking as his riders went down under wounded mounts, tangling up more of his lines.

That's when the lightning started. I spotted a man standing in the saddle, calling down bolts on my men. They were thrown from their saddles or blown to bits by the explosive concussions. Craters marked the streets where they struck.

I reached out and quashed his ability through the Empyrean. He threw a furious glance my way, then was swept away in the charge of men. Cavalry from the front, dragoons from the rear.

His forces broke, and my own got to the messy work.

Men fled for the river, some taking their chances with the muddy waters. They were soon swept away by the current. Others tried to force their way through my troops, and were slaughtered for their effort, or stymied by fire.

A detachment split off and headed my way, and I called to my men.

"Ready!"

Fletcher's men spurred their horses, their leader hanging at the back. He raised his hand, tattoos glowing as they approached. I unlimbered Kent's old rifle and called out as their horses gained the base of the hill.

I sighted Fletcher through the glass on Kent's rifle. I couldn't do two things here—it was either hit him with a Null and lose my shot or shoot him and sacrifice a few men. Once again, it seemed an easy choice. Lives were cheap when they weren't family.

Someone on the line got jumpy, and the crack of shot filled the air, smoke billowing out. Lightning cracked down in response, sending the hair on my arms jumping. I cursed and dropped the rifle, stopping the Caller's magic. Too late, several men were blown to pieces, or fused to their mounts.

A piece of a rifle that had exploded when the lightning hit it emerged from the smoke, whipping in what looked like lazy circles. No time to dodge, I felt it hit, just below my ribs, tear through my coat. It ripped into my skin, sent a wave of agony through me. It punched out the other side as easy as a needle through thread and hung there.

I doubled in my saddle, coughed, and vomited. The pain was intense. I moved Threader back, the movement jostling the chunk of wooden stock and sending my intestines roiling.

I reached into my pack and pulled out a bottle of whiskey I'd liberated from the barracks at the prison and drank until numbness spread over me. Then I surveyed the battlefield.

Fletcher's side had taken a heavy blow as well, and over the groans of dying men and the screams of wounded horse, I heard him sound the retreat. They hesitated for a moment, more hoofbeats bringing up the rear.

The remains of my cavalry had mopped up his dragoons and spurred into his rear. I saw him light out, whipping his mount to a froth, tearing away across the plain. I cursed again, too tangled in my regiment to give chase.

The remains of his forces were caught between us at the top of the hill, and the marauders at the bottom. They wheeled helplessly, then the lines met, and we slaughtered them to a man. I personally saw to the Caller, sweeping his head from his shoulders with the saber Bear had gifted me. For a time, I only knew the blade and the harsh cries of men I'd wounded or killed.

When it was over, there were maybe a hundred men left, all mine. They milled about, wiping sweat, blood, or soot from their faces. Most of them stared at nothing, a long stare that said they'd reached the limit of their life and didn't care to revisit it.

When it comes down to it, when it comes down to killin' and taking what the world owes, most men will never step foot on that path. Others will only walk it so far and find they've no more heart for it.

I knew then any of those men could have put a bullet in my back.

I knew then none of them would.

The fire had caught well in Chorn, and the city billowed smoke like a pile of autumn leaves set aflame. I looked to the east, to a dwindling speck. Bear and Ox had disappeared in the press, and I felt no urge of loyalty to find their fate. My man was fleeing. I turned my mount, and with a quick snap of my heels, spurred him after.

Fourteen

Alone again. The few men who might've followed wanted no more truck with me. I'd led half their number to their deaths, and the rest I'd abandoned. I'd like to say I felt bad about that, but I knew Fletcher rode for the capitol now, knew he had to ride across the Waste. I rode as fast as I dared, but both myself and Threader were tired to the bone, and I knew we had little left. Finally, with vultures circling in the sky, drifting in and out of the smoke over Chorn, I rode to the river.

I washed the smoke and stink of death off myself, tending to the wood in my side carefully. When I thought I had the wound clean enough, I ripped the wood free. A gout of blood and clot came with it, spilling out in a red-black tide. Dizziness overcame me for a moment, and I swayed, threatened to fall. I held still until it passed, and then tore up strips of shirt, stuffing them into each end. When that was done, I wrapped one more around my stomach to hold it in place and called it good enough.

I spent the rest of the afternoon tending to Threader. He'd been ridden hard, but in all was hale. I affixed a feedbag and brushed his coat and mane while he chewed contentedly on oats. I took stock of my possessions—a pistol, the saber Bear had given me, two knives, and a few days' of food and ammunition. I refilled my waterskins in the river and bedded down for the night near the banks.

I lit a fire to keep the scavengers at bay and prayed the wind would stay steady in the other direction. So far, I'd been fortunate to avoid the worst of the stink from the carnage nearby. I slept in fits and starts. The smell of death clung to me, and my mind made a grave of it, recalling the way Ginny had rolled into the dirt when we buried her. I woke crying out, the sound echoing across the plain, swallowed by the rising sun.

I saddled up Threader and rode into Coldharbor. I knew that, like me, Fletcher had to stop here on his way through the waste. There were wayfinders here, men and women who could navigate the desolation. I wanted a hot meal.

The people in the streets were skittish as Threader and I entered town. They cast fearful glances at the black smudge in the sky, just a few miles off. Some made the sign of their god, others squinted and blinked, maybe hurried their steps. None seemed to think a lone man was responsible.

I rode to a pub, broken down, a little out of sorts. The sign over the door read The Dripping Bucket, the wood cracked from the sun, peeling. This close to the Waste, the elements spared no one and nothing. It was like winter had never been known here, and most everyone walked around with skin tanned like leather.

I stepped inside. It smelled of stale beer and body odor.

Small tables sat in near-dark, and a barmaid delivered beer like she was doomed to do it for eternity. I sat, ordered food and a drink, and when they arrived, tucked in. When I finished, I sat back and stared into nothing.

What's the plan here, Cutter, Ginny would have asked. Whether it was turning a field or building a fence, those were the words she spoke. She knew I needed to think things over. Whether it made a difference, I didn't know. I'd always been good at killing. Kind of shit at anything else.

So, I sat back, and I thought. *What's the plan here, Cutter?*

I knew Fletcher was already on his way across the Waste. A part of me wanted to let him go, let the sands swallow him. That part was small and suborned by the pang of jealousy that went up at the thought. No, Fletcher was mine. I intended to see it through. I knew a little of the landscape of the Waste from before. Before the Church had turned on us.

There was a little town out there once—Clews—I could ride hard, maybe lie in wait in the ruins. And after, I could go home. *Or,* another part of me said, *you could ride to the Capitol. Open a gate wide. You know the stories. Of Nulls who gave their life to tear the Emypyrean.* I wondered what Ginny might think of that. Would she approve? A man did for his family. A man provided, protected. And I thought that if I couldn't do either of those things, the least I could offer was vengeance, no matter the cost.

I'd been lost in my thoughts when the girl approached. She was slight, a little on the malnourished side, if I was honest. She sat down at the table and rolled up a sleeve, showing me the scars around her wrist. A Burn. At the end, the Church had figured out how to shut us off from the Empyrean entirely. It explained why she looked half-dead.

"Heading east?" She asked.

I nodded.

"Need a guide?"

"Aye," I said. "How much?"

"What you got?" She asked.

I dug in my pouch, laid my cash on the table. She made it disappear.

"Got a name?" I asked.

"Riley."

"Get your shit, Riley. We're heading out."

She eyed me for a moment, as if she thought I might die in the chair. I probably looked it. In time, she simply nodded, and left. I didn't wonder at the simplicity of the interaction. Burns weren't known for their fondness for life. They'd been hollowed out, cut off from their gift. Most didn't survive much past the process. Others simply spent the rest of their meager lives barely living.

I finished my beer and laid money on the table. Threader waited outside, and I mounted. I looked back to the west, to where my home had once lay. To the past. Smoke clouded the sky.

Riley joined me before too long, a pale mare beneath her. She just nodded.

I wheeled my mount and spurred him through the east gate.

The Waste screws with a man's head. The places you ride through might be grass one moment, desert hardpan the next. The mirage shimmer of deadlands are everywhere, and oftentimes the size of lakes. And there are other things. A pack of spiders with the faces of men scurried across our path once. They called out as they chased a six-legged lizard.

"Ten for a dime! Sixteen for a penny!"

"Spare the blood, spoil the vicar!"

"Nine! Nine! Nine! Nine!"

We changed our path, then halted the horses abruptly. We'd nearly rode into a deadland watching the oddities. We picked our way carefully through a narrow strip where another rose to the left, and once free, rode hard and fast again. We stopped at midday to feed the horses and give them water from one of the skins. I took a bit of dried lizard and some foul-smelling cheese while leaning against a boulder that had sprung up from nowhere. Riley hunkered down beside me.

"You got business in the capitol?" She asked.

"Not as such."

"How's that?"

"Followin' a man. If he happens to lead me there, that's where I'll end up."

We chewed in silence for a moment. She spoke up again.

"Might be I'd want to visit."

"Yeah?"

"Yeah. Might be I'd want to speak to some men there."

I looked at her. She met my eyes, didn't look away. There was something both hard and dead there. I understood. The Burn takes away more than the magic. I took another bite of the meat, and night fell like someone had dropped a curtain while I was mid-chew. I frowned.

I knew the Waste held some nasty surprises, but had no idea just how broken it was. I had little time to think on it. Stalkers, once not there, now there, crept from the dark. They wielded wicked knives and short scythes.

As soon as they spotted us, they moved with a speed I'd never seen from the creatures. In a matter of moments, they were on Threader, razor teeth worrying his flanks. Three charged me. I kicked one in the stomach, and it reeled back.

Another came from behind, and I felt its teeth tear into my shoulder, even though my coat. I screamed and pulled one of the short blades from my back, leaving it in the thing's guts.

The two still standing had already closed, one swinging his blade. I turned and took the edge on the meat of my triceps. The coat stopped most of the cut, but I still felt the steel bite deep, and hot blood rolled down the inside of my sleeve.

I fell back and pulled the pistol, firing off four quick shots. The beasts fell. Threader was screaming, rearing up and kicking. Two of the stalkers lay nearby, heads crushed. Another poked at the horse with a spear. Somewhere to my right, Riley screamed in rage, the wet sounds of knifework following the sound.

I shot the stalker in front of me down and leapt into the saddle, more of the beasts emerging from the night. Riley killed her own assailant and followed suit. We spurred our mounts, hooves tearing up dirt as we fled, the sound like hammers on bone. More rose up as we rode, and I emptied the pistol into them, Riley laying about her with a cavalry saber.

When the pistol's hammer fell on empty cylinders, I pulled my own blade free and got to cutting, the weapon slashing a path for us before my hand grew numb from the wound in my arm. It fell from my fingers, lost on the path.

Finally, we broke free, and still I rode Threader until his breath came hard and lather flecked his flanks. I looked back. Stalkers lay in gory puddles behind us, dwindling steadily. Threader stumbled, pulling my attention back to the present. I slowed him, dismounted. He stumbled again, went down to one knee.

I checked his flank. It was boiling with maggots, the wound suppurating. Something in the stalker bite. I spared no thought for my own wound. Whatever poison they carried, I was likely immune to since eating their flesh.

Riley dismounted, came to look herself. She looked up from inspecting the wound.

"Right. Only thing for it."

She made it back to her horse and waited.

Threader whinnied, a low pitiable sound. I stroked his nose until he lay down. Then I reloaded my pistol and put a bullet in his head.

The pistol cracked, and night flashed to day again. I gathered my things and slung the saddlebags over my shoulders. When I was sure I had everything, I turned, trying to find my bearings.

There, not three hundred feet away, a cluster of worn buildings, the color of ash. I'd found Clews.

The town was empty. Not just abandoned, but devoid of life. It looked as if someone had built the buildings and left it as it was. We found the saloon and climbed the stairs to the second story. Silence dogged my footsteps. I took time to strip my coat and shirt, tend to the wound in my arm. It had started to ache, but it showed no signs of the corruption Threader's wounds had.

I wrapped a strip of cloth around it, hoped it would hold. Infected or no, I'd lost blood, and my hand ached. I could barely close it. If I wanted to do any more shooting, it'd have to be left-handed.

I sent Riley to get water from the pump if there was any to be had. When she was gone, I lifted my shirt. The bandage around my middle was gore-stained, drying to black. The meat around the wound was raw and had begun to smell of almonds. I pulled it free and tied a fresh one, my breath coming in hissing gasps.

I ate more, and despite myself, slept. The night was blissfully devoid of stalkers, but not dreams.

It was hot. *Damnable hot*, the Sherriff would have said. Not that I approved of such language but looking at the dust occasionally swirling in under the saloon doors, I thought it apt. I sipped at my beer and watched the man across from me fidget with his pocket watch. It was gold, the case worked with an intricate scroll. The man's fingers were deft and made the watch walk around his palm and over the back of his hand, then into his pocket and back again. The man flipped it open and scowled at the time, as though he could cow it into changing in some way, then closed it again and resumed playing with it. I looked up at his eyes and the sweat beading on his forehead.

"Tell me," I said.

The man across from me, Burton, was lean. His eyes showed a bit too much white and were bloodshot, but they were sharp. He sat in his chair with an ease that belied his hands, the midday heat in the saloon not fazing him. Occasionally, a patron walked through the doors and bellied up to the bar, and Burton's eyes followed them, tracking like a hawk might track a mouse. His free hand hung over the back of the chair he leaned in, hand close to the big gun he wore on his hip. It was an Imburleigh, like the officers wore in the war. He flipped the watch over and over in his free hand for a moment, then heaved a sigh and looked up at me.

"I 'ent crazy, so you know," he said.

I shook my head. "I'm not here to make judgments, Burton."

"Aye, 'spose so. Still, I can't have an officer thinking I'm crazy when what I need is absolution. Why I liked Chalmers. He 'us a good 'un. Listened and kept his opinions to hisself. Judge not lest ye be judged—you know that 'un?"

I nodded. "I know it well," I squashed my impatience, "What's troubling you?"

"Didn't used to be much of a godly man," Burton began, "Nowadays, I believe, but I'm not sure I can forgive Them."

I let a slight frown crease my forehead. "You think your gods have wronged you?"

"Aye, but not before I wronged Them."

"So, it's a punishment," I said.

"Aye, but not as you'd think, and harsher than that, too."

"What do you consider harsh, Burton?"

"You wouldn't believe me," Burton said.

I eyed the man and wondered if I was being strung along. I hadn't the time to be played for a fool and didn't cotton much to being taken for one. Burton shifted in his chair and checked his watch again, tongue reaching out and touching his lips tentatively. I thought that, then again, maybe the man was simply uncomfortable telling another man what was obviously a deeply held belief. I also thought it possible the man hadn't called me here to debate theology.

"Why did you call for me, Burt?" I asked.

Burton picked up his beer and took a long swallow.

"Ent never confessed before now. Figured it might make things different. Maybe get me some forgiveness."

"Here?" I asked.

He looked around. It wasn't a booth in the Church, but it was as close to private as you could get in town. The tables were spaced a fair distance apart, and the men who were there talked among themselves in low tones. It was too early for carousing, and most of the barmaids were still off shift. I leaned in, elbows on the table. Then the other man took a deep breath and began.

"I'm not a bad man, Captain. You see, I ent got nothing against nobody that ent got it coming. I ent never killed a man that didn't need killing. Except...," his eyes shifted to his watch, and the saloon doors. "It 'us the Cutler boy. Had to have been four, mebbe five years back. I was walking the boards here—back then I 'us the night watchman. Sherriff was off in the Creek, or Benton - I forget.

"Anyway, I had just made my round when I stopped at the depot—'usn't much back then, just a set of rails and a saltbox. I remember the moon was big that night, and the stars was tossed across the sky like sparks when Gemmel's hammer hits that anvil of his. The desert was quiet—seemed like sommat had scared off the coyotes, and all you could hear was that wind scraping across the desert, like a knife on stone.

"I'm ashamed to admit this, preacher, but I 'us scared that night. The Gantry boys had been seen just a few miles west—big boys, and mean, and accused of everything that rhymes with rape and murder. So there I 'us, smokin' my pipe and watching that sky, and I hear something behind me. Sounded like a footstep, like someone sneakin' up, like a thief in the night.

"I called out. I says 'Hey if you're there, let me know.', and they didn't say nothin'. So, that sound comes again, and I say again, 'Hey, let me know you're there. I got this Imburleigh, and I don't wanna shoot ya."

I stopped him. "Why didn't you turn around?"

Burton's eyes looked wet. "I 'us afraid. No man wants to see his end comin', and I figgered if it were the Gantry boys, let 'em shoot me down while I was lookin' at that sky."

I nodded. "Go on, Burt."

Burton heaved another sigh and continued. "So I calls out a third time. I says, 'Damn it if yer gonna shoot me down, do it, ya yellowbelly.' That sound came again, and I'd had it. If he 'usn't man enough to end me, I'd end him. I drew, and spun, and shot him dead in the eye.

"Wasn't 'til the smoke cleared that I saw what I'd done. There was the Cutler boy, dead as a doornail in the street."

Tears rolled down his face. "'Usn't my fault, preacher, you gotta believe me! That boy was deaf and dumb, and prone to wanderin'."

"What did the court say?" I asked.

Burton sniffed and wiped his eyes. He took another long swallow of beer and tried to get himself under control.

"They said 'usn't my fault. I couldn't have known if it was a Cutler or a Gantry, and since the boy was touched, I might've just done him a favor."

"You ever do anything for the family?"

"Aye, I paid for the boy's burial."

"How'd they take that?"

"Not well. The mother, she 'us never a talker. Now she barely utters a word. The father, well, he's never forgiven me."

He seemed about to say something else, but just then the bell over the schoolhouse chimed once, loud and deep. Burton looked down at his watch and closed it, then put it away. He stood and straightened his clothes and his gun belt, then tossed a few coins on the table.

"Thanks for the time, Captain. I've gotta be going."

He walked to the saloon doors and hesitated. He looked back and called to me.

"You should come, Captain. I might need rites."

I realized what time it was. High noon. I stood and paid for my drink, then met Burton at the door. After a moment, we walked through, Burton into the street, me taking up position outside the saloon doors. Outside, the sun was harsh and high and threw the world into stark relief. Dust eddied and whirled in little devils, and here and there men and women shuffled up against storefronts or into buildings, seeking shelter. A little way down a man stood tall in the sun, his shadow long before him. He wore a gun like Burton's and looked ready to use it. He called out.

"You ready?" He asked.

I could just make out his features—it was the Cutler man.

Burton just nodded. They stood, frozen in readiness across from each other. I imagined I saw the sweat trickling down Burt's face. I pulled a handkerchief and wiped my own. Time seemed to stretch, each moment an eternity, each eternity an infinity. Somewhere further down the road, leather on a harness creaked.

The bell tolled, true noon. The men moved in a blur, their hands reaching for iron, their fingers twitching. There was the sound of thunder, and smoke filled the air.

A body hit the ground, and when the smoke cleared, I saw it was Burton. The man lay with his pistol beside him, the iron glinting in the sun. A red pool spread from under him, turning the sand and clay to red mud. Down the street, Cutler holstered his weapon and walked away. I went to the dead man.

His eyes were fixed open, the pupils pinpricks. He stared at the sky, the blue above indifferent to him. I reached out and closed his eyes, then checked the man's breath with a small mirror. No mist marred its surface. I took the small book of Rites from my pocket and began to read.

"Forgive us O Lords, as we forgive those who trespass against us—"

A gurgling gasp beside me interrupted my reading.

Burton sat up, features contorted in pain. He clutched his chest, and his free hand grabbed my shoulder. His grip was painful, and his eyes frenzied.

"No forgiveness. NO FORGIVENESS," he wailed.

I fled.

I woke. Dreams are strange enough things in a normal place, in a normal life. I shuddered. I had no desire to sleep again in the Waste, could I help it. Something about that place took a man's heart, the deep parts, and twisted it. Maybe we'd done more than break the land. Maybe we'd brought damnation to it.

I looked around. Riley was gone. Must've gone out for sommat or other.

The sound of hooves caught my attention, and I risked a peek from the glassless window. Fletcher rode at an easy trot down the main street. For once, the strange geography of the Waste had worked in our favor, twisting him up behind us while we gave chase.

He looked worse the wear for his trip. His clothes were bloody and soot-stained, his face drawn. If I didn't know, I'd guess the man was in some sort of pain. Suited me fine.

He saw Riley before she'd noticed he was there. She was coming back, bucket in her hand. Moonlight spilled over her. Her head was down, dark hair like a veil. He drew—fast and fluid and gunned the woman down. She spun once and fell, the bucket landing upright in the dust.

A pit of rage welled up in me, overflowed. All the wrongs

the world and this man had handed to me came boiling up, hot and blazing.

The world is full of stories of men who've done brave deeds. Faced down their accusers. Fought their oppressors. Planted themselves beside the river of truth, and when told to move, refused. They come into the street, and eye the villain, and there's a showdown. A scrap. A heroic moment. Maybe a bit of witty speech. This was none of those.

I fumbled around until I found it, then propped the pistol on the windowsill. My left hand wasn't as steady as my near-useless right, so I needed the solidity. I sighted down the iron.

Then I shot him in the back of the head.

I watched his brains spray his horse's mane, watched him slump from the saddle. And I counted it as a job well done.

Because at the end of the day, one kind of dead is as good as any other.

I made my way downstairs after, and hitched Fletcher's horse to the rail outside the saloon. Then I sat on the floor inside and ate a little, watching his corpse. The sun sank, and nothing came out to claim it but the flies. I settled my back against the bar, so I could see the entrance, and dozed there. I needn't have worried. Nothing stirred in Clews, and it seemed nothing wanted to set foot there.

Finally, with the moon high, and even the flies on Fletcher sleeping, a black caul over his face, I slept. Dreams crashed into me like waves from a shore.

She's there for you when you step from the pines, your feet wet, the soles plastered with needles, and the detritus of the forest clinging to you like flotsam in the sea. She wraps you in a towel, your skin cold and damp, the towel warm from her body heat, the nap rough against your bird's chest and too-sharp shoulder blades. She tucks you under her arm, a mother bird taking in her fledgling, and you can feel the softness of her stomach at your elbow, her breast at your cheek. It's one of your first memories, the forest quaking behind you like a birthing goddess, your pulse loud in your temples. She looks down and smiles and her teeth are needles, her eyes pinpricks in the black of the sky.

You shudder and wake, coming from the dream like a bird flinging itself from a cliff. You fall, fall, fall, and then—wake, the room dark, the sheets cool and wet. The desert sits patiently outside your window, the rock and dust as ignorant of the moon as they are of man. You rub your hands together, the remnants of pins and needles dancing their way across your dry skin, and you reach for the tumbler on the bedside table. The warm water washes your tongue, soothes your throat, and you stare out the window, the forest superimposed for a moment over the orange and yellow. A blink makes your lids rasp across your eyes; a swallow sends your throat bobbing like a fish coming up for air.

Ginny stirs in her sleep, murmurs a word—it's unintelligible—and shifts. The play of muscles in her shoulder, the lay of her hair, the whisper of fabric over her skin—tiny tremors in your reality, and your heart clenches, a fist of fibers in your chest. You love her. It's not a question. Still, there is doubt. Does she love you? Of course. She's in this bed, isn't she? She's still in your life. And yet the question eats at you sometimes when you lie in the dark. It happens that way, all the questions you can't ask in the daylight tear their way around your head like a pack of hungry wolves, devouring reason and rationality.

You reach out for her, your hand hovering over her shoulder. Do you wake her? Do you pull her close in her sleep and cling? No. Your hand drops. Would she understand? You settle for another sip of water and slip back under the sheet, your back to hers. She sighs small and presses into you, her shoulders digging into yours. Contentment wraps you like a blanket for a while. You sleep.

She shakes you awake—no, that's not right. The room shakes you awake, the neat plaster vibrating on its studs. Ginny is there, and she's shouting something you can't hear, her lips a pantomime of concern. It's so hot, the desert is creeping in, and oh God why did you move to Copper Creek? You kick off the sheets and roll off the bed, landing on all fours, but the desert refuses to let you be. The heat crawls under your skin, and you'd give anything for the cool shade of the pines and the soothing wet of leaves on your feet. A lizard skitters up the wall—not unheard of—and stops, its head hung in a judgmental angle, its eyes burning pits, and you know the desert can see you through it. You stand and shout and wave your arms, and it scurries up and disappears into a bad join in the wall.

Then Ginny is there, and she's holding you, and though you are *so hot*, you let her, because her breath on your skin, in contrast to the hot room, is cool, and her tears are a balm for your fever. Then, her words come through, and you relax, sagging back onto the bed.

"...just a dream, just a dream. Shh. Shh."

You close your eyes and lean your head against hers, and the room is cooling, and you wonder how she could ever love you.

"It's time for a vacation," she says. Then you're riding north past miles of hot brown wasteland, and as you go, flat rock changes. It becomes tall rock dotted with scrub and then taller rock covered with snow, and then finally, blessedly, hills covered in trees, and you don't think you've ever seen anything so beautiful in your life, and you know here you can make it right, the terrors will stop, and she'll love you.

It's several miles in, and a way from home when she asks you. "Did you miss your mother?"

You shrug, your face turned to the forest, the trees throwing shade and shimmer at you. If you look up, the motion of the horse makes the tops look like they're dancing, and for a moment, you're lost in the movement, a ballet of living wood. Then she asks it again, and you have to turn to her, because if she thinks you're ignoring her, she'll get mean, or what you think of as mean, and you don't want to fight, not so close to home.

"I think so," you say.

"Tell me about her."

An image of a clearing, a thousand trees in every direction, green boughs still wet with morning dew, the smell of pine and loam, the squish-crackle of mulch between your toes. Warmth fills your chest, and you think of the woman-but-not-woman who met you when you stumbled from between the boles, the badgers and chipmunks and robins silent for once.

You struggle for the words and settle on "She was kind." She was, after all. Only the men who came looking, the men with their knives and guns and loud, loud dogs were not, and then only for a short time.

"Is that it?" she asks.

You shrug again and then amend it. "You'll see. Easier to meet her."

You turn to the forest, fleeing past your window, and the soles of your feet ache, your tongue is dry. Not long now.

You turn the horses up a dirt path, little more than a rut in the road. After a moment, she stops. Her face scrunches up, her features a fist, and you smile. It's easier now; the closer you are to home, to know you're loved.

"Is this right?" She turns to you and jabs a finger at the map she's brought.

You nod. "Yeah. Just keep going." And she does. She loves you, and she trusts you, and you smile again. So close now.

The horse jounces, and every little scrape, Ginny cringes and lets a hiss out between clenched teeth. "She better be a damn good cook," she jokes.

"I'll have to roll you out of there."

The horse rounds a curve, and the road widens out to a flat drive, packed earth and pine needles, and you're practically vibrating, and when it halts, you leap off, feet skidding in the loose dirt. Ginny follows, laughing a little at your eagerness, and then the door to the home ahead opens, and a woman, plump but not too much, old but not too much, stands in the opening, her smile wide. Her teeth are people teeth for this day, and her eyes a woman's eyes, and she smiles at you, and then at Ginny. They hug on the porch, the overhang throwing them into shadow and mother says something into her ear, and they go inside, leaving you with the forest. You walk to a tree, your hand caressing the bark—just for a moment—and breathe in deep the smells of good earth, and not that blasted hellscape, and then you follow them in.

Inside, they sit across from each other—your mother and your lover—tall glasses of bright yellow lemonade sweating on the table between them. They're chatting in low tones, and your mother pushes a tin of cookies—probably walnut—across the table, and they talk about little of importance while you drift through the house, your fingers finding every dent and rut of your childhood in the walls. In your room, the bed you spent so many summers on, listening to the rain pound the simple roof, smelling the ozone of lightning, is still soft and clean and cool. In the hall, finger paintings you'd done hang in crooked frames. In the closet, the bones of those long gone still sit in neat boxes, away from time and tide.

You make your way back to the kitchen, where your mother is alone.

"Where's Ginny?"

Your mother chews her cookie, her needled teeth puncturing the dough like the blades of a thresher, and she chews, sips her lemonade. She gestures vaguely and then regards you with those pinpoint eyes.

"She wasn't right for you, dear. Dragging you off to that damned desert. Dinner is in an hour. Go play."

You step out the back door and pull off your shoes and your shirt, then place them next to Ginny's body. The forest is so loud here, so close, and you only want to feel it beneath your feet. You look at Ginny, and you wonder—did she love me? I loved her. If she had loved me, she would still be here. She would have fought to stay.

You look at her a moment longer, her eyes staring at you, at nothing. The desert crowds into memory and you think of Ginny alone in that place had your mother sent her away. This was a kindness. Then the forest calls, and you step into the trees. It welcomes you, the wind through the branches the sigh of a long distant lover made close.

It has always loved you.

I snapped awake. A stalker stood in the road, sniffing the air, pacing slow circles around Fletcher's corpse. I pulled the remaining curved blade from my belt and settled in. Before long, it lowered its head and began to eat, tearing the buttons from his shirt in order to get at his belly. The air filled with wet sounds.

I crept behind the thing and slit its throat while it chewed, holding it with my wounded right, my weaker left making a hash of the job. When it was over, I unhitched

Riley's horse and slapped its rump. It bolted into the Waste. I figured that would tide whatever hunger fueled the damnable place over for a time.

My side was wet and hot, and I'd begun to sweat. I tore the bandage free, noticed Riley's body was gone sometime between now and then. Maybe she was only wounded and wandered off. Maybe this place swallowed her up. No matter.

I grabbed the bucket, poured the remains of the water over the wound. I packed it again, nearly passed out. When it was over, I looked east, then west, and made my mind up. I'd come this far. No reason to turn back. I mounted Fletcher's horse. He was a gentle sort and took no offense to the new rider. I left Fletcher to the Waste, which was all the mercy I could muster for him. As for the girl, she'd find her own way. The tough ones always do.

Fifteen

The waste left me alone. Ginny did not. She appeared in regular intervals, each time a vision of horror. Her skin sagged, sallow and waxy. Her eyes were jaundiced. Her lips cracked and dry. Each time she appeared it was only to beckon me on. Each time I wept and followed.

After a day, the boys joined her. Cracked flesh, blackened by flame. Hollow sockets for eyes. Their teeth black and cracked through the holes in their cheeks. They held their mother's hand and stared dolefully in silence.

Before long, they were leading me. I don't know how long I traveled, only that day and night were no longer concerns, my only companion the pain in my guts. I'd a fever in my flesh for the first couple days. When it finally broke, hunger didn't touch me, nor did weariness. There was the path, and my family, and nothing more.

And then, one day, the sun blazing like an inferno, I found myself on a city street. Wide and clean, neat stores and homes. Gardens flourished in a profusion of color.

Everything was built of stone, with slate roofs. The city climbed a series of hills, and there at the peak overlooking the sea, the Church, tall and proud, the stones blue-white, stained-glass windows catching light and breaking it into a riot of color. On every street, a tall lamp to keep the city well-lit. And from each, a corpse swinging from a noose.

They hung like fruit, the ropes creaking in the wind. Not a soul walked the streets. Every last man, woman, and child —those with help—had found the end of a rope. The city was a charnel house. A mausoleum.

I rode to the Church, opened its doors. Priests and Callers festooned the rafters. Behind the Church, a balcony, looking over the sea. Ginny stood there, whole, and beside her, the boys. Fallon, bright-eyed. Carter, a small smile playing on his lips. Ginny let their hands go, walked to me on bare feet. Around her neck, she wore a rope, and when she reached me, stood on tiptoe, kissed me gently.

"Come with me, Wil Cutter."

She took my hand and let me up a flight of stairs, the runner there red and yellow. Another balcony hung above the first, bright bunting flying from the rail. She undid the rope from her shoulders, tied it for me. I took it from her, felt the rasp of the fibers across my palms. She helped me fit it around my neck, secure it to the rail. She leaned in.

"Do you love me?" She asked.

"Yes," I choked back a sob. "Yes, always."

"You'd do anything for me?"

"You know I would."

"Then leap. Love is a leap, Wil," she said. Her lips were warm against my ear. "Leap for me."

I climbed the banister.

Looked out to the sea.

I turned back, drew her close. I knew what I'd brought into this world when we broke it. There's no one war doesn't touch. No toll too high. I pulled the pistol, jammed it under her chin, and pulled the trigger.

Then I leapt, tearing open a gate as I went.